Monday

Erin Curran

The Seven

© 2024, Erin Curran

ISBN: 978-1-0369-0068-7

Front cover image by Maria Spada
Book formatted by Nicole Hayes

Dedicated to those who never doubted me, those whose support never wavered, and belief never weakened, after all these years.

Contents

PROLOGUE

Castlebrooke

1896

THE AIR WAS THICK WITH THE STINK OF SMOKE. It
was a smell he was well adjusted to. It was a foul smell, but
simultaneously an addictive one. He wanted to greedily suck it
all in while also wishing to stick his head out of the window to
get some fresh air into his lungs. He supposed either way it didn't
matter. He wasn't going to be getting Cancer any time soon.

"So, do you speak Spanish?"

Ophelia was standing at the entrance to the bathroom, pale
skin illuminated by the dull yellow glow from within. The

offending cigarette was balanced between her fingers, hanging dangerously from her hand like an accessory. Her head was cocked with interest, a playful smile on her thin lips.

Matthew frowned; Ophelia's question had thrown him off. "What?"

"I assumed from your caramel skin tone that you were Latino," Ophelia explained. She crossed the small room and climbed into bed beside Matthew. "I was just wondering if you spoke Spanish or not."

Matthew lifted his hand from behind his head and examined it. He barely noticed being in a different body anymore. He had grown so used to being so many different things, he sometimes forgot that he changed at all. Matthew sighed and shook his head. "No, I don't speak Spanish," he answered.

"Shame," Ophelia sighed, lazily lifting the cigarette to her lips, and taking another puff. "I love Spanish."

"Sorry to disappoint," Matthew said briskly.

Ophelia smirked. "You didn't disappoint. It just would have been a nice addition."

Matthew looked to the door of the hotel room and chewed his lip thoughtfully. The wood had splintered from when she had slammed it, the trail of clothes that led from there to the bed exposing exactly what they had been doing beforehand. He didn't regret it. He never did. Even though it was highly looked down upon by society. Matthew wasn't known for caring about what society thought anyway. It came with the territory.

He watched the wisps of smoke that filtered through the air from the tip of Ophelia's cigarette, further polluting the room with its stench. Ophelia herself seemed unbothered by the ungodly smell. Matthew guessed it was maybe because this room wasn't exactly five-star or the fact that neither of them was paying for the accommodation.

"When must you leave?" Matthew asked her.

Ophelia shrugged. "My husband doesn't return until next week if that's what you're asking," she replied. "You have me as long as you want me."

Matthew didn't know how he had wanted her to answer him. He could have done without the reminder that she was a married woman. He wasn't foolish enough to believe that Ophelia herself would wish the same. He had gotten to know her enough through the night to know that she was a hard woman, a reckless woman. Her husband could walk into the room right this moment and she wouldn't even attempt to cover her naked body.

"I don't commit to more than one night," Matthew told her.

Ophelia snorted with amusement. "I see," she answered. "That's one way to make a woman feel cheap."

"Do you really worry about such things?" Matthew asked.

Ophelia didn't need to answer; the smile on her face was answer enough.

"When must you go, then?" Ophelia asked.

"I don't know," Matthew honestly informed her. "Before sunrise, at least."

Ophelia exhaled and stubbed her cigarette out on the tray by the bedside table. "May we at least get one more in before you go? If I really must squeeze myself back into that awful corset only to return to an empty home tonight at least make it worth my while."

Matthew couldn't help smiling. There was a reason he liked this woman. She was like him. Unsatisfied with life, looking for people and activities to make her forget. Ophelia may have been a hard woman and a reckless woman, but Matthew was a reckless man. They dealt with their demons by seeking the intimacy of others.

He opened his mouth to answer but was cut off by the phone ringing. Matthew nearly fell off the bed in surprise. Telephones were still so new; he hadn't gotten used to the shrill trill of the device when it was activated. Both he and Ophelia had been surprised to find that their dingy little room even had one. They were reserved for businesses and richer folk, not a cheap hotel on the border of Castlebrooke.

Ophelia pulled a face and reached across the bed to answer it. "Yes?" she asked. A second later, she was passing the phone over to Matthew. "It's for you."

Matthew took the phone from her with a frown. "Hello?"

"Matthew."

Whitney. How did she know where he was? He thought he had covered his tracks well.

"What is it?" Matthew asked.

"Matthew, we need you. It's important."

Matthew looked to Ophelia, who was watching him with her large, green eyes. "How important?" he inquired.

"Vital. Sybil found him. She found Friday's Child."

CHAPTER ONE

MATTHEW HAD NEVER SEEN SYBIL LOOK SO PALE. The leader was almost transparent as she paced the large sitting room. It made Matthew wonder what she had seen when she found the one that she suspected to be Friday's child. She was mulling something over, waiting for the right time to speak.

It had been a while since they had suspected someone of being one of them. Matthew found it difficult to believe that it had been five years since they had rescued Titus. How had it been that long? Time flew by so carelessly when the minutes didn't mean much. When your body doesn't age, a year could just as well be a decade and it wouldn't make a difference.

"Can you hurry up and say something?" Thursday cut in. "Your silence is making me angsty."

Sybil didn't stop pacing. Thursday groaned and slumped in her chair. By the looks of her, Thursday had been preparing for bed whenever this meeting had been called. If her lack of clothes meant anything anyway. Then again, this was Thursday, she gave as much of a damn about what society deemed appropriate clothing as Matthew cared about what they deemed sexually ethical. At least he wasn't the only person who had been inconvenienced by this meeting.

"What makes you think that they are Friday's Child?" Titus asked, ever the diplomatic one. Matthew couldn't tell what he had been up to before the meeting had been called. Titus rarely left the mansion. Public opinion on Titus' people didn't change overnight. It was sickening, but factual.

Still, Sybil said nothing. The roaring fire by her side bounced off her bright orange hair, giving the impression that her entire head was engulfed in flames.

"Have they displayed abilities that mortals couldn't possibly have?" Titus pressed.

"Can you at the very least confirm they were born on a Friday?" Whitney asked in her usual monotone voice.

"How do you *know*, Sybil?" Matthew himself threw in. He trusted Sybil's judgement more than anyone else's in this room, but she couldn't just call them here with such a claim without giving them some sort of reasoning for it.

Still, she said nothing.

"Jesus, Sybil, say something," Thursday complained, earning herself a dirty look from Titus.

Sybil finally stopped pacing and looked up from the floor. "Where's Sawyer?" she asked.

"Not here," Thursday flatly answered.

"We don't know," Whitney said.

Matthew rolled his eyes. "Shocker."

When it became clear that their abilities weren't just coincidence, and the six of them correlated with a different day of the week, they had agreed. A set of rules was created to ensure that they were all on the same page. One of them was that when someone called an important meeting, they all showed their faces. Especially if it concerned the obvious missing member. If their abilities truly were what they believed them to be, then there had to be seven of them, not six.

Sawyer, however, never adhered to anyone's rules but his own.

Sybil ran a frustrated hand through her hair and leaned back against the mahogany fireplace. Thursday made an ugly noise at the back of her throat. "Just tell us already, you can fill Sawyer in when he stumbles into bed tonight."

At first, Matthew figured that Sybil's relationship with Sawyer meant she was softer on him, but it didn't take long to disprove that theory. He really shouldn't have thought otherwise. Sybil kept her professional and personal life separate, and any time Sawyer broke their rules, she treated him just like she would anyone else. It must have made it awkward when they went to bed at night, that was for sure.

"I'll be kicking him in the jewels next time I see him, that's for sure," Thursday added. "If I had to haul my ass out of bed for this damn meeting, he should be doing the damn same." Matthew couldn't be sure, but he could have sworn he heard her mutter, *"Prick,"* under her breath.

Sybil sighed. "Alright," she conceded. "I went to the Circus at the start of the week to reach out to an old contact. I was told that they were indisposed and that I would have to wait until the end of the show to speak to them. So, they gave me a free ticket and I sat in on a performance." Sybil cast her eyes to the ground. "Friday's Child is one of the performers."

"Male or female?" Matthew asked.

"Male," Sybil answered.

"How can you know he is the right guy?" Whitney asked.

Whatever colour that had remained on Sybil's face drained away. "The rhyme, what does it say for Friday?" she asked.

"Friday's Child is loving and giving." Matthew had heard enough of that damn rhyme that he chanted it in his sleep.

Sybil nodded. "They made him heal. That was his act. *The Man Who Can Heal Anything.*' And he can. He does. I saw it. If that isn't the manifestation of loving and giving, then I don't know what is."

Thursday snorted. "How can you be sure that it's true? I mean, circuses are a con, at best. How do you know it wasn't all smoke and mirrors?"

"Remember the laceration I got last week when those criminals attempted to break into the mansion?" Sybil asked.

"That massive gash on your back?" Matthew frowned. Sybil nodded. Some idiots had attempted to break into the mansion the previous week in search of riches, instead, they were met with six people who had the force of an entire armada. "What about it?"

Sybil turned so her back was to them and untied her nightdress to expose her shoulder blades. Where there had once been a massive cut down the line of her spine there was now nothing. Nothing but pale, freckled skin. Matthew blinked and shook his head, just to make sure that his eyes weren't playing up. No, the wound was gone. How was that possible? It had been deep enough to leave Sybil bedridden for days; deep enough to scar. Now it was completely gone.

"The wound ripped open when we were escaping," Sybil explained as she re-tied her nightdress. "He insisted that he heal it. And he did."

Thursday straightened in her chair. "There's not even a scar anymore," she said.

Sybil shrugged. "He told me he would wipe it clean."

That did sound like some pretty damning evidence. There was no way a mortal would be able to remove a wound of that severity so quickly. A healer. Friday's Child was a healer. This was amazing news. Not only were they a force to be reckoned with now, but they also had someone who could heal any wound they received.

"Where is this Jesus man then?" Thursday asked.

"We are not calling him that," Titus snapped, clearly having enough of Thursday throwing around the 'J' name like it was nothing.

"His name is Finn," Sybil replied flatly, clearly not appreciating Thursday's joke either. "And he's not here."

"Why not?" asked Whitney.

Sybil investigated the fire, her expression grave. "We got separated. I think he was caught and taken back to the Circus. I need one of you to come with me to get him again. If there are two of us there the chances of losing each other lessen."

Immediately, Thursday's hand was in the air, but Sybil politely ignored it. Thursday was determined when it came to missions and she was one of their hardest workers, but when the mission involved running around in the dead of night trying to recover someone, she wasn't the most reliable to stay on task. Thursday's brain was like a pendulum, constantly swinging from one extreme to another.

Matthew already knew that Sybil wouldn't ask for his help, either. His ability wouldn't add much to the mission. His ability didn't add much to any mission. The only times he was ever called on for personal missions was if someone needed to be distracted. He supposed that was what his ability was designed for. It was better than being completely useless.

"Preferably you, Whitney," Sybil eventually said, casting her gaze on the blonde girl who was perched on top of the pool table. "Your ability is one of the strongest. We need that where we're going."

Thursday snorted derisively. "It's a *circus*. How bad could it be?"

"This circus was different. It wasn't elephants and bearded ladies. I think most of the performers are held captive." Sybil looked up from the flames. "The things they were making Finn do for the show, it was abhorrent. Chopping off the limbs of animals and even humans and making him heal them back."

"I'm assuming you're going to burn that hovel to the ground, then?" Matthew couldn't imagine that Sybil was going to let such a cruel establishment remain standing. Especially since they had caused harm to one of their own.

"That's why I need Whitney," Sybil answered. She sunk into the chair closest to the fireplace and rested her head in her hand. Despite being immortal, Sybil always looked like she'd aged half a decade when she was stressed.

"Was anyone else at this circus gifted, like us?" Titus asked. "Any of the performers? We could have been wrong about there only being seven of us."

Sybil shook her head. "No, no one else seemed to have supernatural abilities. Just a bunch of contortionists and people with physical deficiencies. No, I'm pretty sure Finn is the only one of us left."

Whitney jumped off the pool table, the skirts of her dress brushing the wooden floor as she straightened. "When do we go?" she asked, folding her arms.

Sybil exhaled reluctantly. "I suppose we should go now. The sooner we get him out of there, the better. I've never delayed before and I don't intend to start now."

Matthew watched their leader heave herself out of the chair again. The way she moved sometimes; it looked like she was carrying a physical burden on her shoulders. It could be the weight of her responsibility. Matthew couldn't pretend that he understood the extent of the stress overseeing the six, now possibly seven, of them did to Sybil. It was one of the many reasons why he respected her so much. He couldn't do what she did. Not in a million years.

Sybil moved to the door, Whitney following her. At the last minute, she turned around and said, "If Sawyer comes while we're gone, fill him in, okay?"

"No problem, boss!" Thursday replied, sticking her hand in the air, fingers arranged to resemble the word 'ok.'

Once Sybil and Whitney were gone, Thursday was immediately on her feet. Despite the fire blazing away, drowning the room in a warm glow, the shadows favoured her as she twirled across the room to Sybil's chair. "So, she found him, huh?" she sang, jumping into the chair and crossing her legs. "The *final one*. Sounds like he's got some skills, too. Real messiah-like."

Titus sighed heavily from somewhere behind Matthew. "Okay, I'm gone. I refuse to listen to your sacrilege."

Thursday's eyes followed Titus' exit, a mischievous grin playing on her lips as he kissed his crucifix. "Tell God I apologise!" she called after him.

Titus made sure to slam the door in response.

"Someday, he's going to stuff that crucifix down your throat and I'm not going to help you fish it out," Matthew told her.

Thursday blew a raspberry and shrugged. "I'd like to see him try! He needs to stop being so sensitive about his precious God. Everyone is so amped up about it these days."

"So, naturally, you make it your job to insult the majority?" Matthew quirked an eyebrow at Thursday, whose cheeky grin betrayed her.

"Oh, who cares! Titus knows not to take me seriously!" Thursday waved off. She flipped her dark hair over one shoulder. "So, what were you doing before this meeting was called? The usual?"

Matthew slouched in his chair. "Pretty much," he sighed.

"Who was it this time?"

"A woman named Ophelia."

Matthew heard an odd tinkling sound, and he realised that Thursday had tried to hold in a snicker. Clearly, she found Ophelia's name amusing.

"What did you look like?"

To any outsider, the question would have seemed odd. Thursday was the only person who ever had the guts to ask him. The others treated it like some sort of insult. Like the fact that he changed his appearance so frequently and uncontrollably was a disability instead of his gift.

"Someone Latin, I think. She asked me if I spoke Spanish," Matthew answered.

This made Thursday chuckle. "If only your gift made your language transform, too! We could converse in my mother tongue, and no one would be any the wiser!"

Matthew's eyes fell on the fire. Whitney must have lit it, as there didn't seem to be any matches around the hearth. The heat stroked his skin, blistering hot even though he was sitting a good distance away. He sighed. "She was married," he said.

There was a pause. Matthew waited for Thursday's response patiently. He wouldn't dare tell anyone else but her. Sybil would disapprove; Titus would start preaching about infidelity; and Whitney would have no problem displaying her outright disgust. As for Sawyer... Matthew wasn't in the mood to get a lecture about how the 'gifted' and the humans should not mix in such a way.

"What a witch," Thursday eventually chuckled. "But, hey, not your problem. It's her marriage, not yours."

"I knew beforehand, though, and it didn't stop me," Matthew pointed out.

Thursday shrugged. "Don't worry about such things, Mattie. If it makes you feel better, then who cares what the consequences are? Ophelia is the one wrecking her marriage, not you."

Matthew didn't say anything. Any decent human being would have said no the instant they noticed Ophelia's wedding band. Matthew didn't try to act like he was a decent human being, he knew that what he did was pathetic and desperate. However, he needed it. It was like there was a part of him that needed to be assured that he was desirable, even if it meant donning a different face. The thrill of the nights he spent with people like Ophelia was the only thing that made him feel this, whether they be married; courting; single; male; female…

He had come to terms with the fact that if he ever wanted to be desired, he would have to change. He'd even come to embrace it. Matthew didn't think there would ever be a time when he wouldn't need to wear a disguise to capture the attention of others. It was the curse of his gift.

"Oops, am I late?"

Sawyer stood in the doorway, looking not one bit bothered by his tardiness. Matthew rolled his eyes. "No, you're really early and the others haven't arrived yet," he answered.

"Still tragically unfunny, I see," Sawyer answered, sliding into the room. Matthew tried to decipher what the man had been up to that had caused him to be late, but there was no real clue in his appearance.

"Yeah, well, you won't be so snarky in a minute when you find out what the meeting was about," Matthew sneered.

"Oh?" Sawyer threw himself into the chair Thursday had previously sat on. "Why's that?"

"Sybil found Friday's child, Sawyer," Thursday answered.

As predicted, Sawyer stopped smiling. He seemed to tense on the spot, his frame going rigid as the news sank in for him. "How? Where? Who is it?" he asked, one question toppling over the other in the rush to get out.

"Sybil went to some travelling circus and that's where he was. Some healer by the name of Finn," Thursday summarised, picking at her fingernails with disinterest as she explained. "She and Whitney are away getting him now."

"A *healer?*" Sawyer's tone was filled with amazement. "Truly?"

"He healed Sybil," Matthew said. "Got rid of the wound on her back from when those idiots broke into the house. Not so much as a scratch was left behind."

Sawyer jumped to his feet, excited. "Don't you see what this means?" he declared.

"Uh, Friday will make a top-notch physician?" Thursday guessed.

"It *means* that we can't die!"

Matthew stared at Sawyer. Surely, he was joking. "Sawyer, I know it's difficult to remember these things, but I feel I must remind you that we are immortal. We're not going die anyway."

Sawyer spared Matthew an unimpressed glance before turning back to Thursday. "Our only weakness was that we could die from wounds. A gunshot; a knife; an accident. If Friday's Child is truly what you describe, then we're invincible. Nothing will stop us."

"There will be some sort of catch, there always is with our gifts," Thursday answered. "There will be a limit to the healing ability or something that is deemed unhealable, wait, and see. I wouldn't pile all your cards into one deck just yet."

Sawyer wasn't put off by this. That insane gleam that he always got when he was plotting appeared in his eyes, the flames from the fire only extrapolating it. Matthew felt uncomfortable, as he usually did when in Sawyer's presence, and stood up. He walked around the chairs towards the door.

"I'm getting some rest before they return, you should do the same," he said, haphazardly waving behind him as he left.

As the door swung shut behind him, the last thing he heard was Sawyer saying, "Just you wait, Thursday. We'll be Gods yet."

~M~

Matthew was awoken the next morning by Thursday's voice. Her bedroom was right beside his, so he had gotten used to her being his alarm clock. With Thursday, there were two extremes: Either she slept in all day, or she was up at the crack of dawn. When the latter occurred, Matthew could never sleep in. She made sure of it.

"Hey, Mattie! Want to meet the healer? Haul your butt out of bed, then!" she shouted from next door.

Matthew groaned and slung himself out of bed. His eyes and limbs were heavy and tired. He hadn't been sleeping well for the past week. Each night when he closed his eyes, it felt like only moments before he was opening them again or he was being awoken by Thursday's voice. He didn't even dream any more. Every night was beginning to feel empty and hopeless.

He had just managed to pull a pair of trousers on when Thursday burst into his room.

"Hurry up!" she snapped, grabbing a shirt off his floor, and dragging him from the room.

"What's the rush?" Matthew complained, awkwardly buttoning his shirt as he followed Thursday down the hall.

"They're waiting on us," Thursday answered.

They passed the sitting room. Matthew looked over his shoulder at the receding door and then back to Thursday. "Where are they?"

"The infirmary."

Panic flushed through Matthew like a virus. "What? Why? What happened? I thought this man was a healer, what need is there to be at the infirmary?"

Thursday shrugged and didn't answer him. That explained why she was in such a hurry. She wanted to know just as much as Matthew did about why they had to meet this healer in their infirmary. Sybil had implied that the only thing this guy couldn't heal was something that could instantly kill, so what in the world had caused them to need to go to the infirmary?

No one had died. Matthew was sure he would have felt it. He didn't know how to explain it. The seven of them were put onto this planet for a reason, there had to be some sort of connection between their souls. It didn't feel right that one of them could just die. Then again, death was the only certain thing about life. Immortal or not, even Matthew knew he had an expiration date. All of them did.

They hurried down the spiral staircase to where the underground infirmary was located. Thursday didn't even bother to knock before bursting into the room. Matthew followed her, kicking the door shut and closing the final button on his shirt on the way in.

The first thing he noticed was that the privacy curtain had been closed around one of the beds. Thursday was conversing with Sybil and Titus on the outside. As he drew nearer, what they were talking about grew clearer.

". . . is resting. Setting the place on fire took a lot out of her," Sybil was explaining.

"What about him? What about the healer?" Thursday asked.

"Will you lower your voice!" Titus hissed. "He's right there!"

Thursday looked over her shoulder, at the privacy curtain separating them from whoever lay beyond. She immediately spun around. "What? Here?" she said, pointing to the drawn curtain. "Fantastic!"

Thursday disappeared behind the curtain before anyone could stop her.

"Hello!" her voice boomed from beyond.

Sybil groaned and slid behind the curtain to ensure that Thursday didn't overwhelm Finn before he had settled in. Titus rolled his eyes, the coffee-coloured orbs landing on Matthew a moment later. Just noticing for the first time that the shifter was there, Titus tilted his head. "You look exhausted," he pointed out.

"Thank you," Matthew flatly responded. "It's the new look I'm going for."

Titus, unimpressed as usual, passed Matthew as he left the infirmary. He paused as they crossed paths. "Remember to approach him carefully, will you? It's overwhelming when confronted by..." Titus trailed off, unsure of how to politely word his sentence.

"Me. I get it," Matthew answered.

For once, there was no sarcastic lilt to his voice. Matthew was working with Sybil on ways to hide his ability, but progress took time. Someday he hoped to be able to instantly flicker back into his ordinary form, so no one would notice a change had even occurred, but until that happened, he had to choose his locale carefully.

They currently lived in a society where openly expressing your desires was considered uncivilised and improper. Having to suppress the rush of emotions being faced with Matthew's shift usually caused most to pass out. Due to this, he usually chose to stay indoors and only went outside when he was looking for someone to, well, *interact* with.

"No need to sound so bitter," Titus said, glancing at Matthew out of the corner of his eye. "Sometimes I think you need to be reminded."

Matthew squinted at Titus. "What are you talking about?"

"I'm talking about last night. Do you honestly think you can fool me? Don't you realise how immoral your actions are?" Titus pressed.

"Oh Jesu-*Jeez*"-Matthew could practically feel the acid through Titus' gaze as he corrected himself- "Save the morality for someone who will respect your words better, alright?"

Titus' hand went to his chest, where Matthew knew a crucifix lay beneath his shirt. "Fine. I'll do just that."

As Titus left, Matthew felt like if he rolled his eyes any harder his eyeballs were going to disappear into his skull. It was nice that Titus was outwardly expressing his concern for once, but the attempted lecture was unneeded. Matthew couldn't count the number of times Titus had tried to lecture him on his *immorality*. Matthew didn't know if it made Titus feel like a bigger person whenever he lectured others about topics like their morals or faith, or if he genuinely wanted to save people, but he just wished that Titus would understand that in Matthew's case, it was wasted breath.

In a way, Titus' dedication could be admired, but Matthew wished he would put that dedication to work on someone else. Maybe Thursday. Or even Sawyer. Both were just as if not more immoral than Matthew. However, every single time it was Matthew who got the pleasure. To be fair, this could be because he wasn't insane. Trying to converse with Thursday and Sawyer sometimes was like trying to talk to a brick wall. More wasted breath.

Matthew looked at the privacy curtain. Might as well get this over with.

He grabbed the white cloth and gave it a shake. "I'm coming in," he said.

"Oh, right," Sybil's voice came from the other side. "Finn, about Matthew, you know how I was saying we're all gifted? Well, Matthew's ability can be kind of overwhelming"-

Matthew slipped past the curtain and immediately caught eyes with the man on the bed. He expected to feel the usual shivers down his arms and back, instigating the change. He was lucky that the change was painless. If he was able to feel every cell in his body turning over and changing, then he would not have survived the process. Then again, would that have been all that bad? At least then he wouldn't have the burden now…

Except it didn't come.

"Hello," Finn said, holding his hand out for a shake.

Matthew simply stared dumbly at Finn.

He hadn't changed.

Not a single cell in his body had flipped, not even the colour of his hair had changed.

CHAPTER TWO

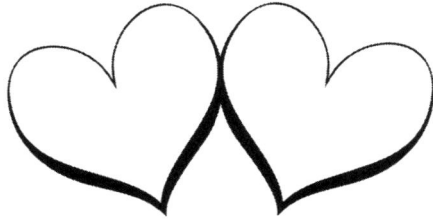

THURSDAY EXPLODED INTO LAUGHTER. Finn looked alarmed at her outburst, his gaze tearing away from Matthew to stare at her in fixation. Matthew felt released without Finn's eyes on him. It was like an immense weight had been lifted off his shoulders. He turned haplessly to Sybil.

"I didn't change," he told her.

"I noticed." Sybil looked as baffled as Matthew felt.

"Am I broken?" There was a pitch of fear in Matthew's voice. The sort of pitch that came with being faced with the unknown. His ability was a burden, but it was a burden he had lived with his entire life. He didn't know what he would do with himself if it just suddenly disappeared.

"No," Thursday's voice cut in. "You're not broken. The healer here clearly likes you as you are."

"I'm sorry, but what are you talking about?" Finn looked the most lost out of the four of them.

"Matthew is Monday's child in the same way you're Friday's, as we were explaining," said Thursday. "He's a shifter. When you first lay eyes upon him, he's supposed to shift into your idea of 'perfect beauty'. Logic dictates that you should be gaping at the equivalent of a succubus right now. Or an incubus, depending on what you're into."

Finn blinked, slowly digesting what was being explained to him. Matthew didn't know if he was going crazy or not, but it looked like the healer's face had turned a couple extra shades of pink.

"Thursday, you shouldn't use such improper definitions," Sybil scolded.

"What? Is it because I implied that he could be attracted to males?" Thursday cocked her head. "Matthew didn't change, so obviously he is attracted to males. Logic is logic, no matter what age we're in."

"I can only apologise for Thursday," Sybil told Finn. "She spent a large portion of her childhood in an asylum, and she has never quite been able to understand formal etiquette or what is considered proper mannerisms."

"My time in the asylum had nothing to do with that; I was like this before I was even admitted," Thursday proudly declared, jabbing her thumb into her chest.

Matthew was watching Finn. The healer's head was constantly moving between Thursday and Sybil, depending on who was talking. He had a very unsure look on his face. He didn't look offended by Thursday's implications, which was strange considering the times they were living in. Not everyone was as open-minded as Thursday or even Matthew himself.

Finn caught Matthew's gaze. He smiled feebly and held his hand out again. "I don't think we've been introduced. I'm Finn."

This time, Matthew didn't gape at Finn's hand like a moron. He accepted the gesture and shook it in welcome. "Matthew," he replied. "Some people call me Mattie."

"Your eyes are very unique," Finn said, gesturing to his own bright blue eyes in reference.

For the first time in his life, Matthew felt sheepish. Normally, he would have a cutting remark or a smart quip on hand to respond to such a compliment with. Not now. He was drawing a complete blank. He rubbed the back of his neck awkwardly and shrugged, "Ah, thanks. I mean, it's not something you see every day, that's for sure."

"Genetic abnormalities have always fascinated me," Finn replied.

"Gene-what?" Thursday interrupted.

"Genetic abnormalities. Matthew has heterochromia, for example. Differentiation of the iris colouration causes both eyes to be distinct from each other," Finn explained. "It's most likely passed down from your parents, or your parents' parents, *or* your parents' parents' parents."

"It has a *name*?" Matthew asked. He had always figured he'd just been born with some weird disease that didn't affect him because of his immortality.

"Everything relating to the body has a name."

"That explains why you didn't change then," Thursday concluded. "He likes genetic whatsits. There, mystery solved, we can all go home."

"*Thursday*," Sybil hissed in warning.

Matthew wasn't listening to either Thursday or Sybil. His attention was wholly and completely on Finn. The man intrigued him. Not only because Matthew didn't change in his presence, but also because Finn seemed to be incredibly intellectual as well. Most people who knew him wouldn't believe it, but there was nothing Matthew found sexier than a man with a brain.

"You've been bleeding," Matthew pointed out.

There was a red patch on the white covers that shrouded Finn's lower body. Either someone had been drinking wine around the infirmary-and since Thursday had just arrived that seemed unlikely-or the healer had bled on the covers himself.

"Ah, yeah," Finn answered, glancing down at the red stain as well. "I am."

"You *are?*" Thursday snorted. "What sort of healer are you if you can't even stop yourself bleeding on our sheets?"

"Thursday!" Sybil exclaimed. She looked flat-out horrified by this point, clearly frustrated by how rude Thursday was being towards Finn.

Finn glanced at Thursday. "I *can* heal," he said timidly, as if afraid she was going to bite his head off if he said the wrong thing.

"Prove it."

"Finn does not have to prove himself to you, Thursday, in the same way you did not have to prove yourself to me," Sybil reminded her.

Thursday shrugged and proceeded to do what Thursday always did: Something insane and incredibly stupid. Matthew didn't have much time to process what was happening before she turned to the closest wall and smashed her head off it as hard as she could.

Matthew's heart stopped in his chest, and he jumped forward to catch her as she reeled back. Her head lolled on his arm, and she grinned dopily at him. A gigantic welt was already growing on her forehead.

"Thursday!" Sybil shouted.

Matthew's eyes caught Finn's for the third time. There was something oddly comforting about looking into those bright blue eyes of his. Like there was some sort of sedative laced through the cobalt iris, made specifically to lull those who gazed at them into comfort.

Finn sighed and waved Matthew over. "Give her to me," he said.

Matthew hesitantly lay Thursday down on Finn's bed. Finn's hand snapped onto Thursday's forehead, right over the welt that had been swelling from the hit. Tendrils of gold began to seep from between his fingers, washing over the wound like tiny waves. Thursday, for the first time in her life, was silent as the golden swirls worked their magic. And, slowly, the welt began to flatten before completely disappearing, like it hadn't been there at all.

There was a moment's pause before Thursday declared, "That felt like an orgasm."

"Thursday!" Sybil exclaimed in mortification. Matthew had never seen their leader look so scandalised before in his life. "You can't say such things in front of company!"

Finn blushed deep scarlet and looked away from Thursday, clearly embarrassed by her description of his healing. Matthew felt a smile tugging at his lips. He couldn't help it. There was something incredibly endearing about this man.

"Thanks for that," Thursday said, throwing herself into a sitting position on the bed and slapping Finn's arm like what had just happened was the most casual thing in the world.

"Don't mention it," Finn replied, still unable to meet her eyes.

"Why are you bleeding if you can heal?" Matthew decided to ask. It was an elephant in the room and Thursday's act of complete lunacy had dragged out what should have been an easy question and answer.

Finn shrugged. "We were shot at while we were escaping the circus. One of the bullets caught me. Nothing to worry about, though. It's only a flesh wound." He paused his explanation there, clearly knowing there was more that needed to be said but deciding to wait for the question instead.

"Did you not have time to heal yourself, then?" asked Matthew.

"We were in a great rush," Sybil stepped in. "Whitney's fire spread so rapidly, we barely got out of the field alive ourselves." She looked at Finn, a puzzled expression on her face. "You haven't made any attempt to fix the wound since we arrived here, though. You healed our burns; so well in Whitney's case that she fell asleep."

Finn was picking at the blood on the covers with his fingernail as if he could somehow remove the stain simply by rubbing his fingers against it. "I can't heal myself," he eventually said.

"Why not?" Thursday asked. "Don't you want to?"

"I didn't say I didn't want to, I said I can't," Finn answered. "As in I physically *can't*. I've never been able to."

As if to prove it to them, Finn showed them his arm, which was littered with what Matthew could only discern as whipping scars. He placed his other hand on top of the marks and closed his eyes, similarly to how he did when he healed Thursday. Except there was no golden glow. His hand simply sat on top of his forearm, useless.

"There are not enough words to properly portray how wretched that is," Thursday said, her brown eyes fixated on Finn's hand.

"So, can you die?" Matthew frowned.

All of them stopped ageing when they turned twenty years old, but if Finn had such a prominent flaw in his ability, maybe he was different to them when it came to his biology.

"I haven't aged a day since my twentieth birthday if that's what you're asking," Finn replied. "Sybil told me that you people are like me. Immortal, I mean. However, I would say that I am more susceptible to death compared to the rest of you."

"And why's that?" Matthew asked.

It sounded to him like Finn was just like them, so why would he be more vulnerable to death in comparison to the rest of them? They could still die if they were stabbed, shot, decapitated, or hung. Immortality did not equate to invincibility. Death was still an entirely probable scenario for them.

"Well, because I'd heal you all whenever I could." Finn frowned as he spoke, clearly confused by why Matthew would ask such a question.

"You'd do that? Even though you barely know us?" Matthew couldn't keep the disbelief from his tone, despite how hard he tried.

"Healing is what I do. It is my purpose in life," Finn answered. He looked at his hands. "It's literally what I'm made for."

Friday's Child is Loving and Giving.

It made sense. Finn matched the profile of Friday's Child. Mathew had always wondered what power would manifest in Friday's Child, as the description was vague about the entire thing, in the same way it was for all of them. Now that he knew, he couldn't imagine it being anything else. Loving and giving? What's more loving and giving than selflessly healing others without question? Especially without the ability to heal oneself.

Matthew had always thought that he would find Friday's Child hard to swallow. He didn't know why. He had figured it would be another Titus in the making. Loving? To him, it sounded like another overtly religious do-gooder who would wish to lecture him every day of the week about his choices in life and how they didn't correlate with God's word.

He did not expect this. Nor did he expect to become so... fascinated with Friday's Child. Matthew wanted to sit down and have a conversation with Finn, away from Thursday and Sybil and the rest. He wanted to know more about him to get a better insight into his very being. Matthew didn't know why, but he felt like there was so much more to Finn, so much more just waiting to be discovered.

"I suppose it makes sense since you couldn't heal your homosexuality away," said Thursday.

Matthew gave her a sharp look. He knew that Thursday was far from judgemental, she just didn't know how to read a room. She had partaken in same-sex relations for many years as well. Thursday's problem was that she forgot the attitudes of the current world they lived in and thought she could make a joke about everything.

"Can I speak to Finn alone?" Matthew asked, directing the question to Sybil rather than Thursday, because he knew Thursday would adamantly protest.

Sybil and Matthew shared a look. She knew from his gaze what he wanted to do. "Come, Thursday," she said, her voice commanding.

Thursday groaned and threw a petulant look at Matthew. When he offered no aid, she huffed and complied with Sybil's order, following the redhead beyond the curtain and out of the infirmary.

Matthew and Finn remained silent. Finn was avoiding eye contact, his entire face red with shame. Usually, Matthew didn't have a problem with Thursday's openness but when it came to sensitive situations like this one, he really wished she stayed quiet. She always forgot that such accusations could lead to a man being arrested for gross indecency. It wasn't something she could blurt out at will.

"Thursday didn't mean what she said," Matthew said. "As Sybil explained, she's… not exactly all there, if you know what I mean."

Finn said nothing.

"I'm sorry that my ability… did that to you." Matthew was choosing his words carefully. He was finding Finn's silence unnerving, and he was worried that he was saying the wrong thing. "If you're scared that we'd turn you in, we won't. Half of the people in this house are gay. Thursday included. She just has an awful sense of humour. We only have each other, we would never throw you to the authorities, especially not for that."

Finn ran a hand over his face. Matthew noticed more whipping scars on his arms and wrists. It was odd seeing a healer so wounded.

Finn mumbled something, and it took Matthew a moment to figure out what it was he had said.

"Half?"

Matthew nodded. "Half," he confirmed. "Thursday and Sawyer-you haven't met him yet-have interests in all sorts of genders. So do I."

It didn't occur to Matthew until the words were out of his mouth that maybe Finn's attitude towards all this wasn't like theirs. He could have been in denial because he agreed with the general opinion on the matter. Maybe he had an ugly attitude towards people like them and he rejected that part of himself so adamantly that when Thursday called him out, he was stunned.

Finn had fallen back into silence. Matthew held his breath, stealing himself for a fight. He had gotten into fights before, but that wasn't his problem, he just wasn't fond of fighting someone who was already hurt and at an obvious disadvantage. That still wouldn't stop him from punching the healer in the mouth if he said anything unseemly.

"You?" There was a lift in Finn's voice that hadn't been there previously.

Matthew nodded again. "Yes. Me."

"You aren't trying to trick me, are you?" Finn questioned.

The shifter frowned. "Why would I trick you?" he asked.

Finn's blue eyes were weary, cautious, and questioning. "Men accused of such acts are being pulled from the streets and trialled like criminals. Why wouldn't you trick me if you believed such a thing?"

Matthew sat down at the end of Finn's bed and shrugged. "I mean, there's no way for me to prove to you that I'm not trying to catch you out or anything," he said. "But, if I was, or any of us were, don't you think that when Thursday realised what my ability showed in you, we'd have acted in revulsion?"

Finn pulled a face. Matthew wished he could see what thoughts were running through the healer's head. He understood Finn's hesitance to trust him. It was hard to know who to trust and who not to trust with such a huge secret. It was either be open and risk persecution or remain in silence and pray every night that no one figures it out.

Matthew's eyes dropped to the healer's hand, which lay by his side on the bed. He reached out and placed his hand on top of Finn's. Carefully, so very carefully. Like he was made of glass.

Finn's hand was cold, like stone beneath Matthew's fingers. He felt the urge to grip tighter, to warm the skin with his body heat. He wondered if Finn felt cold. He could fetch more blankets or throw wood on the fire if it was needed.

"I haven't done anything," Finn said quietly.

It was clear what he meant: *I haven't acted upon it.*

"I have," Matthew shrugged.

Finn finally looked at him. His eyes were wide with shock. "How?"

"There are ways and means," Matthew explained. "Ways to just get on with it just beneath the eye line of the authorities. It's gotten more difficult since the hysteria that has followed the trail of Oscar Wilde..." Matthew inhaled sharply. He had avidly followed Mr Wilde's case, which had resulted in the author's persecution. "But there are ways and means."

Matthew was surprised when Finn laughed. It was quiet and soft, but he had heard it. "What are you? Some sort of expert?" he asked.

"Monday's Child is Fair of Face," Matthew reminded the healer, gesturing to his face with a flourish. "When you excel at beauty, things like sex become secondary because it is so easy to get."

Finn still looked slightly guarded. "So, you normally change shape?"

Matthew's eyebrows screwed up. "Normally, yeah."

"Why didn't you change for me, then?"

Matthew caught Finn's gaze. Blue met blue and green. The healer still had many walls built up around him, but Matthew could see that he had managed to climb over a few during their conversation. He was usually incredibly good at breaking down people's defences. He did it a lot under the guise of a thousand different faces to worm his way in and gain their trust. However, Matthew hadn't been trying to trick Finn into trusting him.

He couldn't even if he wanted to. He didn't have the guise of a different face, of the face the healer most desired. He was bare. Himself. Purely Matthew. The very thought instilled fear into his heart.

The fact that Finn had started talking to him about this subject was encouraging. It wasn't an easy thing to admit, especially not in these times. Not when it was considered such a threat. Such a pointless thing to be believed to be a threat. The fact that Matthew hadn't turned into a woman in front of Finn exposed the healer to something he could very well have not even admitted to himself yet.

"Well," Matthew began, "that's the question, isn't it?"

CHAPTER THREE

MATTHEW LAY OUTSIDE IN THE GRASS. It was an unbearably balmy day. The sunlight burned through his closed lids, leaving behind a blurry golden glow where there was normally a dull darkness. The grass was still wet with morning dew, but he didn't care. It was the only thing cooling him beneath the brutal sun. Besides, the water would dry.

He had left Finn to rest a few hours previous and hadn't encountered any of the others since. The mansion grounds were massive, consuming acres and acres of land. The entire complex belonged to Sybil. She had never enclosed to him how she had come upon such land, but Matthew had never felt the need to press the issue. It was hers, he had seen the papers, what more was there to know besides that? He was sure Thursday had demanded to know the instant she had arrived, but it had never been information that Matthew felt was important. These people had saved his life, so what place did he have to question the legitimacy of their lodgings?

Sybil's mansion was the size of a large boarding school, the structure shooting so high into the sky that it almost looked endless from the bottom. It was stupidly large to house only seven people, but it had been Sybil's intent from the beginning to provide a home to every one of them. A noble intent for someone of her clear status. Only someone of noble lineage could have a home so grand, yet Sybil had opened the doors to five more people without question. Soon to be six.

Most of them had come from the gutter, yet that didn't deter her. Matthew didn't know how Sybil had made the connection between her ability and the day her birthday fell, but whatever it was that had caused her to make the discovery sparked a desire in her to find the other six. A quest which was, now, complete. There were Seven of them. Seven. They were complete.

Matthew didn't feel complete. He figured that once they had found Friday's Child, he would have felt a form of closure. A sense of conclusion? Anything at all. Instead, he just felt normal. Could that be the point? Their quest didn't finish with a bang or even a whimper. This was what normalcy felt like. This was them.

Now what?

Matthew grimaced into the glowing yellow behind his eyelids. What did they do now? Just live together as a unit? Get on with life like everyone else? It didn't feel right. Surely, there was more to them than just a normal life. They had abilities. Powers beyond human comprehension. Surely, they had to put it to use!

But... how?

He didn't see himself as a do-gooder. He only ever used his ability to get people into bed with him. What other use was there for it? There was certainly no way to utilise it to do good deeds for others. Unless, of course, their calling wasn't necessarily for *good* deeds...

The ethereal glow of the sunlight was suddenly consumed in darkness like the moon had eclipsed the sun. Matthew's eyes snapped open, and he found himself staring up into the grinning face of Thursday, who loomed over him like a mad, smirking giant.

"The grass is wet," she stated.

"What?" Matthew answered. "I wasn't aware."

Contrary to her previous statement, Thursday threw herself into the grass beside Matthew and stretched her legs out before her. The skirts of her dress were wrinkled and tangled around her knees in a mess of blue fabric. Ankle exposure was not at the top of the list of concerns for Thursday.

"I like him," she said, lying back and staring up into the clear blue sky.

"Who?" asked Matthew.

"You know who. The healer. Finn." Thursday cocked her head. "I wonder if he's Irish. Sounds like a very Irish name. Or Scottish. Something Celtic. He doesn't sound it though…" She reached out and slapped Matthew's arm. "So, do you like him back?"

Matthew frowned at her. "What do you mean 'back'?"

"Don't play stupid," Thursday scolded. She turned onto her side and propped her head on her hand, her elbow digging into the wet mud of the ground beneath her. "There isn't some fault in your ability, and you know it. Finn likes what he sees, he doesn't need any change. He wants a piece of Mattie uncut."

If she were talking to anyone else, Thursday would have been slapped into next week for using such improper language, but rude words meant nothing to Matthew. They were just a string of letters that formed a sound. Why would that bother him? Besides, if he even attempted to slap Thursday, he could bet that she would give him a dead leg in return.

He knew what she was talking about, though. Ever since he had left Finn in the infirmary, he had been throwing around the idea in his head that his ability hadn't fluked. Could Finn view the skin Matthew was born in as his personal idea of beauty? If this were true, Matthew didn't know what he would do with the information. Did he leave it? Pursue it? How does one go about proposing such a question to a person they just met?

"I suppose I'm just going to have to get him into bed," Matthew sighed.

This was how he dealt with most of his issues. Need information from someone? Sleep with them. Need something from someone? Sleep with them. Don't understand something about someone? Sleep with them. Sex and seduction were the only weapons Matthew had but he knew how to utilise them well. Even if there had been some fluke in his ability, Matthew was confident that he would still be able to seduce the healer in one way or another.

"That's the spirit!" Thursday grinned. Only she would praise him for such a decision. Not even Sawyer would do such a thing. "I'm sure your lady friend from yesterday will be quite jealous. What was her name again? Opal?"

"Ophelia." Matthew cringed even just saying her name.

In the rush of the past day, Ophelia had become nothing but a far-off memory, if even that. Matthew wondered if she had already found someone else to mess around with while her husband was away on business trips. She had been none too pleased when he had left in such a hurry, leaving her alone in the room with nothing but the job of explaining the broken bed frame. He had left his information with the reception desk if it needed to be paid for, so at least he had done his part there.

"She didn't come off as the jealous type to me," Matthew sighed, stretching his arms above his head. "She reminded me a lot of myself. Just in female form."

"And you slept with her," Thursday concluded. "Narcissistic much?"

"Who better to love than yourself?" Matthew grinned.

Thursday raised her eyebrows. "And you love yourself?" She didn't look convinced. Matthew held her gaze, hoping it would eventually make her believe him.

Thursday was good at picking up on things. Whether it be a quiver of a lip or a falter on a word, if it was there, Thursday would notice it. Matthew didn't know what it was that he had done that made his statement unbelievable, but he must have done something.

Matthew could lie about many things, but it was becoming increasingly difficult to lie about himself.

Throwing her hair over one shoulder, Thursday broke their staring contest first. Matthew wasn't dumb enough to believe that this meant he had won, it just meant that Thursday had grown bored with what they were doing. Beating Thursday at anything was near enough impossible and it was better just to accept it than fight it.

"So, we're *complete*," she said. "There's nothing to do now. The plan had always been to find whoever's left. Now there's no one left. Weird, isn't it?"

Another interesting thing about Thursday: She always knew what he had been thinking.

"At least Sybil's theory was right," Matthew answered. "About the days of the week."

"Did you ever doubt her?"

Matthew shrugged. "She never divulged to us what her reasoning behind it had been, can you blame me for being sceptical sometimes?"

"I didn't have the energy to argue it. I just let her get on. Turns out she was right. Good thing, too. I've grown attached to my name."

Thursday suited her name so much, that Matthew often forgot that she took it up when Sybil rescued her from the asylum. Her real name was Trish. It didn't fit her at all. It sounded too... normal. Too mundane. Too ordinary for someone so bizarre. Thursday was an interesting name. Matthew had certainly never encountered someone named such a thing.

Matthew himself always used the nickname 'Monday' when he visited the local molly house owned by Adelia Day. Adelia was an exceptionally friendly woman who owned the pub beside Castlebrooke Station and often used the expansive area upstairs as a place for people like Matthew to meet. She was careful about it, as were all her male patrons, as they did not wish to get raided. There were many rules to stay safe. The first rule: don't use your real name.

In a way, Matthew was never in any real danger even if he did use his real name. He changed his appearance so often when he was in public, he always looked different from one day to the next. He would never get caught. Still, it was nice to partake in the rules despite this. It made him feel included. Part of the community. Not the outsider he would surely be considered if the truth about him ever came to light. It was common to use names like days of the week or months of the year, so Adelia never questioned when different men would come by under the guise of the name Monday.

"Sawyer is always blathering on about how we should refer to ourselves with our day names," Thursday said, cutting into Matthew's thoughts. "He's a bit too keen on the idea, to be completely honest. He's too keen on all of this... *stuff*."

"Sawyer likes to consider himself more important than he is," Matthew brushed off.

"While that is true, if there were anyone to become important through desire alone, Sawyer would be the one to do so,"

Thursday muttered, her eyes distant as she looked to the sky. "His ability is practically a gateway to it."

"There are things even Sawyer's ability can't give him," Matthew quickly replied.

Sawyer's ability unseated Matthew. There was something about the ability to manipulate luck that made him feel uneasy. Like fate would always be in Sawyer's hands if he truly wished it to be so. This would be alright, in a way, if Sawyer and Matthew didn't avidly despise one another. If Sawyer wasn't so hard-set on his belief that the seven of them were special, he could have manipulated fate to have killed Matthew by now. It sounded irrational, but Sawyer was a madman. Rationality wasn't something he excelled at.

The grass began to rustle and when Matthew looked up, he saw Whitney, wearing her usual bored, I-could-be-doing-something-more-important-right-now expression. "Matthew, there's some woman at the door looking for someone called Samuel," she said.

It took a moment for Whitney's words to process properly in Matthew's brain. He took many names, sometimes numerous ones a day, and trying to recall which name was used for which person could prove to be quite difficult. It didn't take much thinking, though, for he had only just used this name yesterday.

"What is Ophelia doing here?" he blurted out.

Whitney didn't look impressed. "You expect me to answer that?" she asked flatly.

Matthew clamoured to his feet, Thursday following quickly on his heels, egged on by her curiosity. Whitney looked them both up and down, her pale nose crinkling in obvious disgust at the state of their clothes. She turned and started to make her way back up the garden, clearly leaving the situation of their visitor to Matthew.

"How does she know where you live?" Thursday demanded, pursuing Matthew as he followed Whitney's path back up to the house. She didn't struggle to keep up with him, despite his legs being longer than hers and his stride being quicker than usual.

"When Whitney called claiming that Sybil found Friday, I was in a bit of a rush. I may have written down our real address instead of making one up because we broke a bed and I may have needed to pay a bill," Matthew explained. It was stupid of him to have done it, but he hadn't expected Ophelia to come looking for him. "I thought she just wanted a one-night meet like I did, I never expected to see her again!"

"You underestimated your-or should I say, *Samuel's*-charm," Thursday teased.

Matthew would have normally laughed at this, but he couldn't find the humour in it now. Never had any of his past flames come looking for him, especially not in his own home. Sybil wouldn't be too pleased when she discovered that Matthew had given out their address, but right now he wasn't concerned about that. All he was concerned about was getting Ophelia as far away from the house as possible. It wasn't safe here for humans. Not yet. Not everyone had mastered their abilities yet.

Ophelia stood in the foyer, looking as radiant as Matthew remembered. Thursday hung back in the sitting room doorway, no doubt readying herself for some sort of dramatic scene to unfold before her. Ophelia's back was to him, her inky black hair falling down her back in a ringlet of curls, the silky strands a pleasant contrast to her snow-white gown. She was busy admiring one of the paintings that had been passed down Sybil's bloodline. Matthew assumed it was by some sort of prestigious artist, but he wasn't sure who.

He cleared his throat to announce his presence.

Ophelia turned, a puzzled expression immediately embezzling her features. "You're not Samuel," she said carefully.

Matthew was fascinated by his ability sometimes. When Ophelia had first laid eyes on him, he had had no choice but to turn into her fantasy, into Samuel, but now that he had already done so, he was under control of his appearance again. He didn't have to turn into Samuel if he didn't want to.

"Yeah, ah, hello, my name is Matthew. I'm, ah, Samuel's brother," he lied.

Ophelia frowned. "You're not Hispanic," she pointed out.

"No. I'm adopted." In a way, Matthew enjoyed lying. It came to him very easily, in the same way charming people did. He was good with words. When it came to manipulating people, that was.

"Where is Samuel, then? I requested for Samuel's presence," Ophelia asked.

"Samuel isn't here," Matthew replied. "He hasn't lived here in a long time."

"Why would he provide your address on a bill, then?"

"If he was with you, probably to trick you into thinking he lived here," Thursday suddenly piqued up.

Ophelia's dark gaze fell on Thursday as if just noticing she was there. "And you are?" she asked with fake pleasantry in her voice.

"Thursday. Samuel's sister."

Ophelia didn't question this due to Thursday's Hispanic roots, which were made clear through her skin tone and the accent that always tinged her words. They stared at each other for a moment, Ophelia clearly at a loss for a means of speaking back.

"Why are you looking for Samuel?" Matthew interjected.

"We have business."

"No, you do-I mean, what sort of business?" Matthew internally cringed at himself, cursing his stupidity.

Ophelia looked from Matthew to Thursday, then back to Matthew again. "That woman who answered the door, is Samuel seeing her now?" she asked, very obviously restraining the envy in her voice.

The very idea almost made Matthew choke on his words. "Who? *Whitney?* I can assure you that is not the case. Whitney is more like family to him; to us all."

"She's pretty," Ophelia stated.

"Well... I guess."

Whitney often captured people's attention without having to say a word, the classic combination of pale skin and blonde hair enough to enchant anyone who laid eyes on her. Matthew had known her for so long and knew how sullen she was on the inside, so he had never had any interest in Whitney in that way. He meant it when he said she was more like family to him. Like an annoying little sister. She was, after all, his junior by two days.

"There seems to be a lot of pretty women around this place," Ophelia added sceptically, casting her gaze once again on Thursday.

"Did you miss the part where I said he was my brother?" Thursday asked.

For some reason, Ophelia didn't look convinced. Matthew watched her carefully, still completely confused about why she was even here in the first place. He had explicitly told her that he only did one-night meets, and at the time she had seemed to understand. So why was she seeking him out again? What could she want?

"I need to find Samuel, whether he has found another woman or not." There was a sudden desperation in Ophelia's tone. One that quite alarmed Matthew. Even Thursday looked slightly startled by it.

"Why?" Matthew asked.

Ophelia shook her head. "It's my husband. He found out that I slept with Samuel. If I don't find him then he's going to kill us both."

CHAPTER FOUR

"You gave a human our address?"

Sybil's voice practically shook the walls. Or were they actually shaking? Even Sybil didn't know how to completely control her ability. It often manifested itself when she was angry. Matthew winced and directed his gaze to the floor. Even the horse statuettes on the fireplace seemed to be grimacing. He didn't want to meet Sybil's intense gaze. She could burn through steel with her eyes when she wanted to, and Matthew was a lot softer than steel.

"In my defence, I was in a rush after I was told that you had found Finn. I didn't expect her to come looking for me again," Matthew answered.

"That's beside the point!" Sybil cried. "You gave our address to a human who could-and has-come here looking for one of your many personas. Don't you understand how dangerous it is for a human to be here right now? Whitney answered the door, Matthew. *Whitney.* If she hadn't been in such a placid mood, she could have blown the poor woman out of the sky!"

"I'm sorry, alright? I made a mistake!" Matthew insisted. "I honestly didn't think she would come here. I would never have intentionally put her in danger."

"Now we have the trouble she has brought along with her. The trouble *you* had a hand in causing due to your reckless behaviour!" Sybil continued.

"Is it really that much of a problem?" Sawyer, who had been sitting in the armchair by the fireplace quietly up until this point, interjected. "I mean, is the troubles of a human woman any concern of ours?"

Sybil did not look at all amused by Sawyer brushing off the severity of the issue. "I don't know about you, Sawyer, but I couldn't sleep at night if I knew that a woman was killed due to a problem one of our own had a hand in creating."

Matthew knew by the expression on Sawyer's face that he would be able to sleep like a baby at night if Ophelia was murdered by her husband. Matthew himself, however, was on the same boat as Sybil. Even the idea of Ophelia's husband prowling the streets at this very moment looking for his wife and her lover made him shudder. Samuel could hide but Ophelia had nowhere she could go.

Ophelia herself was currently in the foyer with Thursday. It was a bit of a gamble, considering how uncaring Thursday was of social etiquette but Titus was busy with his writings; Finn was still in the infirmary; and Whitney was currently too dangerous to be left alone with anyone. Matthew only hoped that Thursday could compose herself for at least fifteen minutes while Sybil scolded him. He knew she was capable of it if she exerted enough energy into it but for Thursday to put effort into something, she had to be interested in it in the first place. Then again, maybe this sudden turn of events would be just juicy enough for her to be even a little bit curious.

Sybil fixed him with a confused look. "Why did you sleep with a married woman?"

Matthew shrugged. "We both wanted an escape."

Sybil sighed. "Matthew, you can't keep using that as your excuse for bedding people like some sort of... some sort of..."

"Harlot," Sawyer finished.

Sybil inhaled through her nose and flashed her partner a tight smile. "Yes, thank you for your input, Sawyer." She looked back to Matthew. "I understand that you are going through a challenging time, especially where your powers are concerned. We all are, but"-

"But you can go out in public. You can interact with people. You can do anything you wish without constantly worrying about being turned into some ugly hybrid creature due to there being too many eyes on you. The only time I can leave this mansion is if I go out intending to bed someone. It's the only way I can exist without becoming some sort of recluse," Matthew answered.

"Have you tried courting someone?" Sawyer asked flatly.

Matthew looked at Sawyer with disdain. "You know full well I can't."

"Oh yeah, I forgot no one likes your 'normal' face," Sawyer threw back at him.

"Sawyer!" Sybil snapped. "Enough!"

"No, it's fine. Sawyer prides himself on the facts, doesn't he?" Matthew bitterly responded, slouching in his chair. "Can we focus on the problem at hand? What are we going to do about Ophelia?"

Sybil ran an exhausted hand down her face. "Did she mention who her husband was? Is it anyone we could track down and take… care of?"

"We were fornicating, Sybil, she wasn't really in the mood to talk about her husband," Matthew answered.

If he remembered correctly, Ophelia made a point of not mentioning her husband. The only time he ever cropped up was if she was insisting that he was most definitely out of the way and not a threat to their night at all.

"You're going to have to go and ask her, then," Sybil concluded.

"How? I don't look like Samuel anymore!"

"We know full well that you can turn into previous bodies."

Matthew shook his head. "It's not that simple, Sybil! I don't have control of it! Yeah, I have the memory of old bodies but it's not like some picture book, I can't flick between them and try them on like clothes!"

Sawyer sighed heavily; his dark eyes unimpressed. The birthmark in his right eye always looked so malevolent, no matter where it was directed. It made Matthew's skin crawl. "What *can* you do, exactly?"

"Nothing I can convince you is of worth," Matthew muttered.

Sybil turned to Sawyer. "You could try? You're good at getting what you want. You could try to get it out of her who her husband is."

"I wish I could, but I don't think I want it enough," Sawyer shrugged. "The fate I sway always comes from a place of my desire. Human affairs aren't… interesting enough for me. I daresay they're quite primitive in comparison."

"In comparison to what, exactly?" Matthew demanded. "The exciting life that *you* lead?"

Sawyer's head rolled on his neck, and he looked at Matthew with boredom. "Are you still here? You've already proven your worthlessness."

"Sawyer, stop it," Sybil scolded. She had turned bright red like she usually did when she was frustrated. Matthew knew he was a handful, but Sawyer's blasé behaviour always stressed their leader out in equal measure. Sybil was like a shepherd with a bunch of crazy sheep that were constantly fighting one another.

"Look, I'm sure Ophelia won't be reluctant to give us information on her husband if we make it clear that we're going to help her," said Matthew. "I mean, why would she? Who cares where 'Samuel' is?"

"You do have a point," Sybil conceded. "There are six people in this house who are fully capable of protecting her if the need arose."

Matthew shook his head quickly. "Seven. There's seven of us."

Sybil's brown eyes widened. "Oh, that's right."

"About that, when can I meet this new guy?" Sawyer asked. His face looked much more animated now. This topic clearly interested him more than that of Ophelia's troubles.

"The man is injured, Sawyer, he doesn't need your million and one questions treatment just yet. It can wait," said Sybil, waving her hand dismissively. "If we were to help Ophelia, we'd have to attempt to hide that we're... different."

Sawyer snorted and slumped back into his seat. His expression quickly melted into horror when he saw that Sybil was serious. "Sybil, you surely aren't suggesting that we allow human filth into our home?"

"Stop talking like that, Sawyer," Sybil snapped. "Humans outnumber us on this planet, how can they possibly be filth?"

"Filth is common," Sawyer simply shrugged, unbothered by Sybil's anger.

"Sawyer, stop that," Sybil bit back. "I will not take away your right to believe what you wish but please refrain from talking about it in my presence."

Sometimes Matthew wondered how Sybil and Sawyer had anything resembling a relationship. Every time they were together, they either ended up bickering or fighting. They were an extremely mismatched couple. Sawyer believed in some sort of purity in their blood, meaning that anyone different from them was the 'filth,' while Sybil believed that they had a duty to the humans as beings that-while could be considered inferior to them-were equally important. Maybe they had decent debates behind the door of their bedroom, but all Matthew ever saw was... well... this.

But then again, wasn't that what made a couple? Those arguments and disagreements that make you frustrated and full of rage, and the ability to put that aside when night falls, and you climb into bed with one another? Matthew couldn't know for sure. He never experienced such a thing. Ophelia was the first person to ever find him again after a night together, even if she hadn't exactly found the person she was looking for.

The door to the sitting room was suddenly flung open and Ophelia charged into the room. "Why can I hear yelling?" she demanded.

"Thursday!" Sybil barked. "I told you to keep her out of here while we spoke to Matthew!"

Thursday appeared in the doorway. "Oh. No. Ophelia. Don't. You can't go in there. It's a private conversation," she said in a monotone.

Sawyer snickered but Sybil was flustered by Thursday's disobedience. She cast her gaze to Ophelia, who was standing close to where Matthew sat, chest heaving with… anger or fear, Matthew couldn't tell. "We want to help you," Sybil said.

"Where's Samuel?" Ophelia insisted. "He is in danger, wherever he is. I don't care if he's sleeping with someone else, my husband will kill him regardless!"

"Samuel is gone." Sawyer stood up and approached Ophelia. Matthew jumped to his feet also, afraid that Sawyer was going to attempt to hurt her. "He left Castlebrooke late last night. It's what he does. He sleeps with women without regard for their feelings and then skips town." He looked over his shoulder at

Matthew, an evil spark in his dark eyes as he added, "He's a selfish pig of a man."

"The point is, he's gone," Sybil said, pushing Sawyer back. She gently took Ophelia's hands. "We're interested in helping you, now."

Ophelia looked weary. "Why would you care? You're a bunch of strangers."

"You just told us that you're being tailed by someone who intends to murder you," said Sybil. "Do you believe we'd close our door on you upon hearing that?"

Ophelia was already shaking her head. "You don't understand. This isn't a matter that will be solved by a call to the authorities. My husband is on the force. He knows how to… pull strings. Some people owe him favours. He would never be arrested."

"We'll figure something out, Ophelia," Sybil promised. "We won't let you die."

Ophelia drew away. "How can I trust you people?"

"Samuel isn't here anymore but we are," Matthew said firmly. "We aren't going to let his stupid mistakes get you killed."

Ophelia stared at Matthew. Her eyes danced over his face for a moment before focusing intently on his eyes. She had given Samuel a similar gaze the previous night when she was trying to figure out his intent. "You said that you aren't related to

Samuel, but there's something about your eyes… Something I can't place. They resemble his."

"Is it the colours?" Thursday cut in. "The colours usually do it."

"No, you know your brother's eyes aren't like that, surely," Ophelia answered. She shook her head. "No, there's something else. I don't know. A piece of Samuel is there, I just can't place how."

Matthew smiled and shrugged. "I'm adopted," he reminded her.

Ophelia hummed, clearly not believing this. She returned her eyes to Sybil and nodded. "Okay. I don't have any other option, do I?"

Sybil bobbed her head in understanding and started to guide Ophelia out of the room. "I'll show you to one of our spare bedrooms. I will gladly loan you some night garments for when night falls. Don't hesitate to ask us for anything that you need. There are some things I must ask of you, though"-Sybil was cut off as the door shut behind them. She was going to warn Ophelia to stay away from Whitney's room.

Thursday whistled. "Such drama!" she exclaimed with a grin.

There was a moment's pause. Sawyer then announced, "I'm going to the infirmary."

"Why?" Matthew immediately demanded.

"I'm going to go talk to Friday," Sawyer answered. He didn't even bother passing Matthew a glance as he weaved around him and headed to the door.

"Sybil told you not to!" Matthew hated how childish he sounded. Like a kid tattling on their sibling. "Must you always do the complete opposite of what she asks of you?"

Sawyer paused beside Thursday. He leaned forward and kissed her goodbye. Matthew ground his teeth together. He hated when Sawyer behaved this way. He was in a relationship with Sybil, yet he kissed every one of them, at least tried to-like they were all his property in some way. Matthew didn't know if Sybil saw it this way, but she had most certainly witnessed him kissing Thursday on multiple occasions. Maybe she saw it as a friendly means of greeting. Like the French did.

Thursday only let the kiss last a moment before she slapped Sawyer across the face. Sawyer stepped back and rubbed his jaw, a grin on his face. He left without even apologising for his actions.

"Why do you let him do that?" Matthew asked.

Thursday looked at her hand as it slowly turned pink. She seemed more interested in the discolouration than Matthew's question. "I don't," she answered. "I slapped him."

"Surely you see it coming at this point. Why not stop him?" Matthew pressed.

"It is not my job to control Sawyer's actions," Thursday shrugged. "I react as I see fit. If it were anyone but him, I'd probably let them. If I see them worthy, that is."

Matthew, despite his irritation, couldn't help feeling smug at this. "And Sawyer isn't worthy?"

"He could be," Thursday replied. "But he is in a commitment with Sybil."

"Since when have you cared about that kind of thing?"

"Since Sybil forged my mother's signature and freed me from that metal cell." Thursday finally looked up from her hand. "If it were anyone but her my hand would not currently sting." With a shrug and a sigh, she left the room as well.

Matthew stood alone in the sitting room. He stared, transfixed, at the spot where Ophelia once stood. Even Thursday had a moral code of some description when it came to her intimate life. The one who was considered crazy; mad; and unhinged had more dignity in her bed than Matthew did. What did that show?

Matthew was the last to leave the room.

CHAPTER FIVE

**OPHELIA DID NOT LEAVE HER ROOM VERY OFTEN. SHE
MUST HAVE BEEN SPOOKED WHEN SHE WAS TOLD TO
STEER CLEAR OF WHITNEY.** Matthew didn't know what
Sybil told her to justify the warning without exposing the truth
about them but whatever it was must have freaked Ophelia out.
Matthew knew from when he had spent the night with her that
she was not the sort of person to be put off by strangers and she
had certainly been sociable, so whatever Sybil said must have
been enough to make her remain in the confines of her room.

Matthew was relieved by Ophelia's absence. He didn't feel
comfortable in her presence. He felt like he was deceiving her in

some way. She had come to the mansion in search of the man she had spent the night with, and little did she know he was under the same roof as her. Just not in the way that she had thought.

It was ridiculous to feel this way and Matthew knew it. The entire pretence under which Matthew had met Ophelia was deceptive through and through. He had never been forced to witness the aftermath of his actions. He always ploughed on; always going forward; never looking back. A new day, a new face, a new person. Now he had no choice but to witness.

A week after they took Ophelia in, Matthew sat alone in the drawing room. Rain relentlessly beat the window, rivulets of water sliding down the glass like tiny vines rushing to the bottom. He couldn't stop staring at it. He hadn't left the house since Ophelia had appeared. He was tempted to throw all caution away and run into the rain like a madman. He was restrained by the fact that he was wearing his best silk waistcoat.

Matthew could only truly leave the mansion grounds if he was meeting someone for the night. Thursday usually set up dates for him in places where he wouldn't be seen by anyone but his date. Even then, he had to hide himself from the eyes of the public as he made his way to the agreed meeting place. For the past week, Matthew had had no desire to leave the mansion grounds at all. He didn't know if it was because he felt duty-bound to protect Ophelia, or because his heart just wasn't in it at the current time. Whatever the reason, Matthew was not in the mood to change shape. He did not want to be anyone but himself.

A creak drew Matthew's attention to the door. Sybil popped her head around and said, "Hey, could you show Finn around the mansion? He's well enough to walk now. I'd do it myself, but I must go to work."

For a reason he could not explain, his heart lurched. Matthew slid out of his seat, forcing himself to go slow and not look too enthused. "Yeah, sure. Where is he?"

"Just out in the foyer," Sybil smiled. "Thank you."

Matthew found Finn exactly where she said. He looked to be admiring the flower arrangement on the other side of the room, his back to Matthew as he entered through the side door. The healer looked a lot better, the only sign of his previous injury being the cane that he was leaning his weight against.

Matthew didn't even feel like he was walking towards Finn, it was more like drifting, like he was naturally gravitating towards the younger man. He stopped only a step away, pushing up onto his tiptoes and peering over Finn's shoulder to also admire the flowers. Despite the flowers in the vase being peonies harvested from the garden, the scent that Matthew caught was of the violet water on the other man's skin.

"Whitney grows them," Matthew said.

Finn was startled by Matthew's sudden appearance. His shoulders jumped, and he spun around like he had been caught doing something he shouldn't have been doing. He didn't expect Matthew to be so close because when he turned, he bumped straight into him. Finn practically jumped on top of the table that housed the flowers in surprise, his face flushing bright red in embarrassment and his cane clattering to the floor.

"Pardon?" Finn panted, still seated on top of the table.

His voice was a couple of pitches higher than usual, and Matthew had to bite back a smile as he explained. "The flowers. Whitney grows them. There's a patch of grass around the back of the mansion where she does her gardening."

"Whitney is the young woman who aided Sybil in my escape?" Finn asked.

Matthew nodded. "When she's in a neutral mood, she can control the earth. She spends most of her time gardening when she feels such a way. It's the only part of her ability she can control."

"It's strange how you speak so casually of these abilities. I spent my life thinking I was the only one who was... different. It was so abnormal for me. How does one become adjusted to the discovery of six others?" Finn brushed his hair back out of his eyes, and it almost immediately fell back into place.

"It takes getting used to," Matthew admitted. "We all had adjustment periods, it's completely normal. Hopefully, if all goes well, you will begin to view us as family. The seven of us are the only people in this world who can understand each other. In different ways, of course."

Matthew dipped down and picked Finn's cane off the floor. Flicking it around so he gripped the bottom end, he offered the handle towards the healer. "I trust you're feeling better?" he asked, offering his free hand to help Finn down onto the ground.

"Yes, thank you," Finn replied. He gripped the handle and accepted Matthew's offered hand without any hesitation. "I've experienced worse."

Despite what he said, Matthew didn't miss how Finn winced when he slid off the table. Yet once he was back on his feet, he smiled broadly at the shifter. The action itself caused Matthew's insides to heat up. Not in the manner he was used to, either. He was used to all kinds of heat. The heat of the moment; the heated throes of passion; the heating of two selves with nothing but their breath… This didn't feel like that kind of heat. It felt more… innocent.

Now that he was standing facing him, Matthew was able to fully take Finn in. They were almost the same height, Finn only standing an inch or so above him. Gone were the dirty, bloody rags he'd arrived at the mansion in. They had been replaced by a white shirt and black pants that Matthew recognised to be Titus.' The sleeves of the shirt were rolled up to the elbows like Finn was expecting to be called to perform surgery or fix a car at any moment. Most noteworthy, though, were his bright blue eyes, which glistened under the artificial light above their heads.

Matthew had always been told that his own eyes were unique and special. Yet he found more beauty in those two thick cobalt rings framed by thick, fair lashes than he ever could in his own.

"You clean up well," Matthew said. This didn't even feel like a line. He genuinely meant it. It felt like an understatement.

The red returned to Finn's face. "Sybil has been so kind to me. You all have."

Matthew shrugged. "We look out for each other. Even Whitney and Titus, despite how much they will try to make you think they don't care."

"I will return your kindness in any way that I can," Finn said with determination.

Matthew smiled. "I believe you." He gestured for Finn to follow as he headed for the stairs. "Sybil has assigned me the job of showing you around this monster of a house."

"Yes, she said she had work," Finn answered. "It is admirable for a woman of her status to choose to work. Most women who have lodgings of this size and such wealth would choose not to. I hold a lot of respect for women, but I find it most sad when they have no choice but to be an accessory to their rich husbands."

Matthew chuckled. "I'd like to see the man that would try to make Sybil his accessory." Even Sawyer hadn't achieved such a thing, despite his efforts to convince her to quit her jobs.

He looked over his shoulder and realised that Finn needed some time to get up the stairs. Matthew felt foolish for charging ahead and hopped back down a couple of steps to wait for Finn to reach him.

"Where does she work?" Finn inquired.

"The textile factory Mondays to Fridays and then she teaches some rich family's kids French on the weekends," Matthew answered.

"Does she not get tired?"

Matthew lifted his shoulder in a half-shrug. "Saturday's child works hard for a living."

"Where is that from? You said something similar about yourself last week."

They stopped at the top of the stairs. Matthew gave Finn a moment to rest, despite the healer's attempts to hide the pain from his face. The mere fact that he was standing right now after being shot was amazing, so walking was certainly going to be difficult for him. Matthew wondered where the cane even came from. One of the others must have picked it up sometime during the week.

"It's a rhyme," Matthew explained, leaning against the bannister. "It correlates with our abilities. We don't know if it was written about us or if it's just a coincidence, but it checks out."

Finn raised his eyebrows. "What was it that you said the rhyme said about yourself? I can't remember," he asked.

Matthew pulled a face. He rubbed the back of his neck and answered, "Ah, Monday's child is fair of face."

"I see. That's why you allegedly change shape," Finn reasoned, recalling their conversation from the infirmary.

"'Allegedly'?" Matthew repeated.

Finn rested a hand on top of the bannister across from Matthew and smiled. "I mean, I've never actually seen this apparent change of shape take place so for all I know it's a folly."

Matthew could tell from the way Finn spoke that he was joking. He laughed. "I *wish* it was folly. It would certainly make my life a lot easier."

He didn't complain about his ability often. There were people he knew would listen to him and try to be understanding, like Thursday or Sybil, but he didn't see the use in it. No matter what he said, nothing would change. It felt like a waste of words.

"Do you want to know about Friday's child?" Matthew asked, quickly changing the subject before the topic of his ability continued.

Finn quirked an interested eyebrow. "Go on then."

Matthew cleared his throat and put on a theatrical voice as he declared, "Friday's child is loving and giving." He gestured towards Finn's hands and said in his normal voice, "It makes sense. I spent ages wondering what Friday's ability would be. Healing never crossed my mind."

Finn also looked at his hands. "Loving and giving isn't how I would have put it," he murmured thoughtfully. "But I suppose it fits, in a way."

Matthew studied the distant look on Finn's face. Deciding that this conversation was getting old, he offered his arm to Finn and, returning the theatrics to his voice, asked, "Would you like the standard or exclusive tour?"

Drawing his bottom lip between his teeth to stop himself from laughing, Finn threaded his arm around Matthew's and sighed, "Because I've been receiving premium treatment since I arrived here it would almost be stupid not to go for the exclusive."

Matthew's lips quirked up in a smile and he subconsciously pulled Finn closer so that he would lean his weight on him instead of the cane. The smell of violet water filled his senses again. It made his heart flutter in his chest.

Whitney had planted violets in the garden numerous times before and Matthew had never thought much of the smell. He'd even encountered other men who used violet water as a fragrance and, again, it hadn't made any impression on him. Yet,

Finn's wearing of it almost gave the scent a completely different meaning. It was different; fresh; and delightful; simply because of who was wearing it.

Matthew showed Finn around the mansion. It took a good two hours due to the size of the building. There was a multitude of empty rooms that weren't in use but were furnished like they were. It was unsettling, to say the least. It felt like the rooms were waiting for people who would never come. At least one of these once-empty rooms was getting used which they wouldn't have done before last week: housing Ophelia.

Matthew told Finn which rooms were occupied. He made sure to emphasize not to disturb Whitney's room. Not only was the woman incredibly surly every hour of the day but knock on her door at the wrong time and the whole house could go up in flames. It wasn't Whitney's fault. Just like everyone else under Sybil's care, she could not control her ability. She had long, extensive training sessions with Sybil every other day and then remained alone in her room. Matthew knew that Whitney didn't mind, and probably preferred it, he just couldn't help feeling the urge to go and keep her company. Even though he knew that she wouldn't want it.

"The room with the cross on the door is Titus'," Matthew explained, pointing down the hall to the door at the bottom. As he had stated, there was a cross nailed to the middle with Jesus watching over anyone who passed.

"That's actually a crucifix," Finn absentmindedly corrected. When Matthew looked at him blankly, he chuckled. "A cross is just... well, a cross. A crucifix depicts the actual crucifixion of Jesus Christ."

"Titus will like you," Matthew joked. He looked at Finn out of the corner of his eye. "Are you religious?" he asked carefully. Maybe his assumption of Friday's child being another religious man hadn't been too far from the truth after all...

Finn was looking down the hall at the crucifix on Titus' door. "I don't know what I believe," he murmured. "I like to think there's a God out there but after what I've seen, I don't want to believe a God would simply watch and let such things happen."

It wasn't until Finn said this that Matthew remembered where Finn had come from. That gruesome circus that Sybil had described to them. The circus Whitney had burned to the ground. It was a horrific example of the barbaric nature of humanity and the extent they would go for entertainment. Matthew found comfort in the fact that the slaughterhouse under the guise of a circus no longer existed. He hoped Finn did too.

"It's a tricky topic, for sure," Matthew said. He turned Finn away from Titus' door and started walking in the opposite direction. "But there's always a positive to find. Maybe God, if he exists, gave Whitney the fire to destroy the horrors that you witnessed. Or maybe he put Sybil at the right place at the right time so that she would find you."

Finn watched their feet as they slowly made their way down the hallway. "Maybe," he conceded. "Are you religious?"

Matthew choked on his laughter. "Me? Religious? After all I've done? Please. I can't afford to be."

Matthew's reaction made Finn smile. "You don't need a God, just something to put your faith into. We all have faith of some sort. I put mine in healing and modern medicine. You should find something for you to put your faith into. Something that isn't judgemental. That could be all you need."

Now it was Matthew's turn to look to the ground. He watched Finn's feet as they hobbled along beside his own, the cane pressing into the expensive scarlet carpet with each step. Something to put his faith into. He had never thought of it that way but even then, he came up with nothing. He had nothing.

"Maybe," was all he said in response.

Finn an took interest in the infirmary. Matthew had figured that Finn had seen enough of it during his week of rest, so he had intended to just pass by it on the way to the basement. Finn, however, asked if they could go there specifically.

"I thought you would have been sick of this place by now," Matthew explained as he helped the healer into the room. The fire was still going from when Finn had been resting there, giving the infirmary a warm glow that it didn't deserve.

"I didn't get to have a proper look because I was injured," Finn answered.

Finn parted from Matthew for a moment. When their arms unhooked, the shifter felt cold. It was like an important part of himself had detached itself. He stood in silence as Finn hobbled down the aisle between the beds. The healer ran his hand along the wooden boards at the bottom of each bed; brushed his fingers along the blue privacy curtain; and caressed the medical tools on the trolley with his fingertips. He had this expression on his face that was full of awe like he was witnessing something utterly amazing unfolding before him.

Matthew stared. There was something about the pure fascination on Finn's face that he found extremely captivating. He found himself staring at that enthralled face; at the curiosity and intrigue burned into every feature as he took everything in.

Matthew forcibly shook himself out of his trance. "Why would you wish to have a proper look around here? It's just an infirmary."

"It's a place of healing," Finn answered. "I hope someday to be a fully qualified, certified doctor. All of this fascinates me. I can't help it."

Matthew blinked. "A doctor? But you can *heal*."

"My healing is a shortcut compared to what doctors and nurses do and achieve every day," Finn replied. "It makes me feel like I'm cheating. I hope to learn the proper ways of healing…" He frowned. "What do we call those who don't have abilities like our own?"

"Humans," Matthew shrugged.

"I see." Finn nodded. "Well, I wish to learn the proper ways of healing humans. I want it to be my profession."

Matthew found it strange that Finn wished to study to be a doctor when he could fix any wound or disease right in his hands. Maybe it was an ambition Finn had before he even knew that he could heal. Maybe it was simply a dream he didn't want to let go of. Maybe there were reasons why Finn wanted his doctorate that he didn't wish to divulge. Matthew could understand the desire to keep things private.

"So, would you use your ability when you're a doctor?" Matthew asked.

Finn glanced up at Matthew through his eyelashes. "You just said 'when you're a doctor'," he stated.

"Yeah, your point being?" Matthew answered.

"I might not ever get to be one."

Matthew blew a flippant raspberry at such a suggestion. "What are you talking about? Someone who caresses a stethoscope like he's caressing a lover must someday use one professionally."

Finn's hand jumped off the stethoscope at Matthew's analogy. His cheeks turned that endearing pink colour again. "I mean, I just find the instruments extremely interesting. How they work and what they can do and the like. I'm sorry if it came off as strange, we could leave if you want, I just sort of wanted to have a loo"-

"Hey, I wasn't implying anything." Matthew wrapped his fingers around Finn's pale wrist and placed his hand back onto the stethoscope.

Their eyes met. Their eyes found each other often. As if they subconsciously drew back to one another if they spent too long apart. Matthew didn't mind, which was uncommon for him. He believed that staring into a person's eyes was too intimate. The eyes can give away too much and Matthew had never felt comfortable letting his past flames stare into his for too long, even if they were different each time. He had too much to hide.

Yet here he was, unable to tear his own eyes away and, in the process, allowing Finn to stare into him.

Cobalt was growing to be Matthew's favourite colour.

Finn reluctantly broke the spell, casting his eyes downwards. The pink in his cheeks turned to an intense red. Matthew's eyes lazily fell, and he realised that his hand was still sitting on top of Finn's.

With a sheepish laugh, Matthew drew it away. He didn't want to, but he also didn't want to scare Finn away by being weird.

"Ah, what was it you asked me?" Finn asked.

"When?" Matthew blinked very slowly, clearly still very drugged on the moment.

"When you said I was a doctor," Finn prompted.

"Oh. I asked if you would use your ability if you got your doctorate?"

Finn's expression changed. Suddenly serious, he said, "Oh no. There would be no way to heal everyone and how would I choose who is or isn't deserving? I don't have the right to make that kind of decision. Besides, it's natural for humans to be mortal. They die. It's part of their life cycle."

Matthew stared at Finn in disbelief. "You're kidding, right?"

Finn shook his head solemnly. "I know it sounds mad, but it's just something I couldn't do. If someone was shot in the street in front of me? Of course, I'd do what I can to help them. If I became a doctor and worked long hours in a hospital? I couldn't even if I wanted to. I don't wish to make decisions that should be reserved for a God."

The comparison reminded Matthew of Sawyer. Sawyer believed himself to be a God in every sense of the word. Finn looked queasy at the very idea of having such responsibility on his shoulders. Despite only having ever achieved annoying Titus, Sawyer's God complex was something that Matthew knew contributed to Sawyer's madness. It had to. Why else would he be so insane without a medical diagnosis?

"Being a God is overrated," was all Matthew could think to say in response.

Finn chuckled. "I'd like a shot at being friends with this Titus fellow, I doubt that coming in singing that I'm God would help my case anyway."

"Yes, very good point," Matthew grinned. "Although Titus is a bore. Who cares what he thinks of you?"

Finn's eyebrows rose. "Oh? Whose opinion do *you* think I should care about?"

Matthew put his hands on his hips, and he began to wander around the room in fake deep thought. "I mean, if we're talking about life lessons and the grand scheme of the world, I'd say don't care about anyone's opinion of you, but you're smart, you probably know that already. *So,* considering that

I'll assume you mean who in this house aren't bores like Titus."

Finn leaned on his cane, a smile on his face as he watched Matthew hypothesizing. "What would you say if that was what I meant?"

Matthew pivoted on his heel to face Finn once again. "It's obvious. Myself."

"Oh? You didn't give that much thought," Finn laughed.

"I don't need to. I'm a delight." Finn rolled his eyes. "Okay, okay, Thursday is pretty cool too."

"Has anyone ever told you that you're extremely modest?" Finn enquired.

"Is that sarcasm I detect?"

"I don't know, you're the expert here."

The two of them watched one another for a moment. Finn's eyes bored into Matthew, glittering with amusement. Matthew noticed that when he smiled, tiny crinkles appeared near Finn's eyes. Someone once told him that that was a sign that a person's smile was too wide. Matthew never understood the concept of a smile being too wide. Who puts a measure on happiness? He couldn't remember who it was that told him that but if he had to guess it was probably some stuck-up high-society woman who barely cracked a smirk.

Matthew didn't want to say anything that would break the moment. He liked simply observing Finn; studying his face; his eyes; his smile, without interruption. He was unnerved by how quickly he had become entranced by this man, but the unease was not strong enough to make him look away. If it had been anyone else, Matthew would have already kissed them, at the very least.

Usually, Matthew had no problem pursuing the people he desired, but something was holding him back this time. Some sort of invisible force, whispering in his ear that this was different. Finn was different. He had to wait. If he waited, it would be worth it. This wasn't like other conquests. If asked to describe why he thought this, Matthew would be unable to answer. He had no idea. He was willing to humour the suggestion, though. If it meant he could continue to admire the healer's face, then he didn't care.

"What are you doing down here?"

Matthew spun around. His mood immediately soured at the sight of Sawyer standing in the doorway to the infirmary. "If it were any of your business, you'd know," he immediately bit back.

"Matthew was just showing me around the mansion," Finn explained. He slowly made his way over to stand by Matthew's side again. The smile hadn't left his face.

The fact that Matthew couldn't understand anyone smiling in Sawyer's presence made him surprised by this.

"And you took him back to the infirmary?" Sawyer's tone was as stale as the expression he currently wore. His long black hair was combed back from his face, exposing every hostile crease and wrinkle.

Matthew opened his mouth to respond with a cutting remark but was beaten to it by Finn. "I asked him to take me back here. I didn't get a proper look when I was injured so I wanted to return. Healing inspires me." Finn's lips twitched into a wider smile, if that were possible, and he placed a hand on Matthew's shoulder. "Matthew was happy to help me."

"I see." Sawyer's eyes had followed Finn's hand as it had crossed the space over to Matthew. His expression was suddenly unreadable. He sighed. "Matthew, your woman is asking for you."

Matthew's eyes widened, and he felt Finn's hand tense on his shoulder. "What woman? I don't have a woman!"

Sawyer's dull eyes sparkled with amusement. "Ophelia. Don't you remember? You messed up her life and now she must stay with us?"

"How can she possibly be asking for me?" Matthew demanded. He didn't dare look at Finn.

"Well, she's asking for Samuel, but since you're Samuel, you're going to have to answer her request."

Matthew ground his teeth together angrily. He wondered if Finn would find it horribly offensive if he punched Sawyer in the mouth. There was nothing but venom behind Sawyer's words. Matthew wouldn't have been surprised if he went to Ophelia and she hadn't even been asking for Samuel. Now Finn was going to think he was in a relationship. Why did that bother Matthew so much?

"We better go speak to her then, shouldn't we?" Finn said, breaking through Matthew's irritated thoughts.

Matthew stole a glance at the healer. He was met by a tender expression, those beautiful eyes soft and understanding.

Finn offered Matthew his arm, which the shifter wasn't hesitant to accept. Matthew drew the younger man closer once again. It was already becoming a force of habit. Finn wasn't that heavy, and Matthew barely noticed the extra weight as they hobbled to the door.

They passed Sawyer on their way out. His face was indifferent, but Matthew had known the man long enough to recognize when there was something else brewing beneath the placid expression. He had not gotten the response that he had wanted from his attempted sabotage. Matthew threw him a sickly sweet smile on their way out.

As they headed back up the stairs, Matthew heard Sawyer curse him under his breath.

CHAPTER SIX

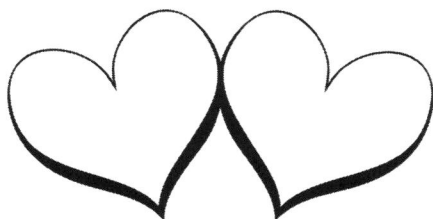

"You're welcome to come along to Ophelia's room if you want. She's not my woman."

Finn smiled but shook his head. They had climbed up to the foyer and ascended the first flight of stairs in silence. It wasn't an uncomfortable silence. Matthew had felt quite contented in it.

"This is your personal business. I do not wish to impose upon that. Besides, Sybil said I could choose whatever room I wanted. I've elected to sleep in the attic. I'm very tired from all this walking around so I think I shall head up there now for a few hours."

Matthew nodded. "Good choice. Away from the madness." He glanced at the ceiling, imagining the many flights of stairs that Finn would have to climb to reach the attic. "Do you need any help getting up there? It's a long way up."

"No, thank you. I don't want to get too comfortable having a walking aid. It will make me lazy," Finn grinned.

Disappointment welled up in Matthew's chest, but he quickly smothered it before it showed on his face. "Good point." He paused. "Ah, don't be afraid to come by if you need anything. I'm always here. I can't leave this place unless it's carefully organised, so I'm usually always around."

Finn bobbed his head in understanding. He didn't ask Matthew why he couldn't leave. Maybe it was obvious, or maybe he simply didn't care. Whichever way, Matthew was glad for it. "Thank you," Finn said. "You've been very kind."

Matthew shrugged. "It was nothing."

The healer smiled and slowly turned on his heel. He gave Matthew one last look over his shoulder, the gaze stealing the shifter's breath just as he had released it. "I'll see you around, Matthew," he said.

"Ah, yeah, see you around," Matthew stammered back, giving a pathetic wave that made him inwardly cringe.

Matthew didn't know if he felt relieved or sad as he watched Finn disappear up the stairs. A lot of tension left his body the instant Finn wasn't in his range anymore. It was now that he first noticed that his heart was pounding in his chest. It was like he had been holding himself tight, keeping himself in line so that he wouldn't say or do anything stupid. Was this what it felt like to care about what another person thought of him? He didn't like it. How did people go through such sensations regularly?

Ophelia's room was in the middle of the first floor. Matthew paused at her door and exhaled. Why was he so nervous? He felt more anxious preparing to enter her room now than he had been when he had entered the hotel room knowing that she was already waiting for him. He supposed it was because he had never pretended not to know someone he had slept with before. Mainly because he never saw them again.

Matthew knocked on the door and waited. Gone was the confident Samuel, who didn't even knock before swaggering into their hotel room. The cocky Spaniard had not even given Ophelia a chance to speak before he swept her up into a kiss. Matthew felt extremely bare, standing on the other side of Ophelia's room waiting for her to let him in. Like an exposed nerve afraid of being poked.

"Come in," came Ophelia's voice.

Matthew inhaled and entered the room.

He had never been in this room before. He had never had a reason to. This wasn't even his floor; let alone a room he would visit. It was decorated extravagantly, with gold silks and warm reds. It was rooms like this one that made Matthew think that this house had to have been handed down to Sybil. This type of embellishment wasn't her style. She was very much a less is more type of person. The room lacked the warmth of being lived in. Matthew didn't know how Ophelia had been spending the week, but it had not involved making her room seem any less... empty.

Ophelia was sitting with her back to the door at a mahogany writing desk beside the fire. The flames flickered off the walls, casting giant shadows across the ceiling and floor. It was the only source of light in the room and since it was raining, that made the room look very dark indeed.

Matthew stood by the closed door awkwardly, not sure whether he should be the one to break the silence or wait for Ophelia to say something first. She was writing something. Her black hair had created a curtain around her face, shielding her words from an outsider's view. Her presence, even when silent, was still extremely dominating. Her very being demanded attention, like no matter what she was doing, she was the most important person in the room. Matthew had adored that about her a week ago. Now it made him uncomfortable.

"I am writing a letter to Samuel," Ophelia suddenly announced, skipping any pleasantries. Matthew felt slightly more comfortable with this. Formal etiquette would only increase his nerves and he wasn't sure how much higher they could go.

"Why? We don't know where Samuel is," Matthew replied.

Ophelia finished her letter with a flourish and turned slowly in her seat. She was wearing one of Whitney's less flattering dresses, yet she still somehow made it look good. That was saying something, since custard yellow wasn't Matthew's favourite colour in general, never mind on clothes.

"I am writing to him in case he ever returns home," Ophelia explained.

"I don't think he ever will," Matthew answered nervously.

Ophelia watched him for a moment, her eyes guarded. "I still wish for you to take the letter. I would feel a lot happier if you did. Just in case."

"Just in case what?" asked Matthew.

Ophelia didn't answer. Instead, she stood and crossed the short distance to her four-poster bed, where she sat down. She gestured for Matthew to sit on the chair she had previously been seated on at the desk. He did as she asked, trying not to look at her letter as he sat down himself. A moment later, it was handed to him.

"Why didn't you just give it to Sawyer instead?" he asked her as he took it from her.

Ophelia looked none too pleased at such a suggestion. "That man unsettles me. He has an extremely uncomfortable presence. He talks to me like I'm beneath him. Typical man. And those eyes... That birthmark of his... It's all rather weird. I'd rather give my letter to a friendlier face."

"Me?" Matthew was confused. Was his ordinary face friendly?

"It was between you or that lovely woman with the red hair." Ophelia brushed a hand through her silky hair and looked thoughtful. "You're a rather strange group of people."

Strange didn't even cover it.

Ophelia did not look at all worried that her statement could have been viewed as offensive. She instead leaned back on her hands, looking thoughtful. "I mean, who calls their child Thursday?"

"Thursday does," Matthew shrugged. Ophelia raised a brow and waited for him to elaborate. "It's not her real name, you see. She called herself Thursday."

The corner of Ophelia's mouth quirked, and she nodded in understanding. "I knew that woman seemed..." She pursed her lips.

"Crazy?" Matthew supplied.

"I was going to say one pumpkin short of a patch," Ophelia replied.

Her description of Thursday was so accurate, that Matthew snickered. "Yeah, that's pretty much her."

Ophelia looked at the canopy over her head. Her pale skin reminded Matthew of the depictions of Snow White from the Brothers Grimm story. Dark hair; fair skin; big red lips. Maybe the Brothers Grimm had somehow envisioned Ophelia before her birth and based Snow White on her. As ridiculous as such a notion sounded, Matthew was currently living as a shifter in a house with a telekinetic; a man with an angel's grace; a woman who could control the elements depending on her mood; another woman who could blast herself into the air with only her hands; and someone who could manipulate fate.

Oh, and a healer.

Somehow, ridiculousness wasn't much of a concern anymore.

"I don't even know why I'm here," Ophelia eventually admitted. "For all I know, you could be more dangerous than my husband."

Matthew shrugged. "You're still alive and it's been a week. I doubt your husband would have been as considerate."

Ophelia laughed at this. "I will admit that you're right about that," she answered. Her eyes drifted to her lap. "He's going to kill me."

"Not if we have our way," Matthew said firmly.

"Why should you care?" Ophelia scrunched her face up in distaste. "I cheated on my husband with your brother. Why should you care if I die or not?"

"While cheating is considered quite nefarious... I don't think it deserves death," Matthew answered. "Besides, Samuel isn't completely innocent either."

Ophelia chewed on her lip, a fixated look on her face. "I assumed he was running from something also, but he never told me what it was. He just said that he needed to escape. I could understand that. I still do. I knew it was for one night, but I didn't expect him to just disappear."

This was why Ophelia and 'Samuel' had gotten along so well. They had the same desire to run from their problems instead of confronting them. They understood one another's need to feel free, even if it was only for a night. Neither wanted to divulge any details as to why they needed one another's company, and neither cared. They just needed to sink into each other and forget their problems and then leave the next morning back to their troubled lives, never to see one another again.

Or so it was supposed to be that way.

She tilted her head curiously. "He had to leave suddenly. Did that have something to do with his disappearance?"

Matthew sighed and lifted his arm in a lazy shrug. "I can't say, I'm sorry. I haven't seen him in months."

Ophelia wasn't surprised by Matthew's answer. Disappointment flickered across her face, but it was there and gone in less than a second. "I should be thankful. Wherever he is, my husband won't be able to find him."

"He won't find you either, Ophelia," Matthew gently reminded her.

Ophelia defiantly lifted her chin. "If he does, I will face him. I cannot run forever."

Matthew sighed. He already knew there wasn't going to be much he could say to convince Ophelia otherwise. He would not let her face her husband, not as he lived and breathed, but there was no use in saying so. Ophelia was the sort of woman who didn't accept help from others often. The fact that she chose to stay here was a miracle.

"I see him in you."

Matthew blinked. "Pardon?"

Ophelia smiled softly. "I said, I see him in you. I see Samuel, somehow. I don't know how. You're both completely different people. Yet there's something about the look on your face when you came to meet me at the door. I can't explain it. You're both entirely different, right down to your eyes." She had begun picking at her dress sleeve subconsciously like she was trying to scratch her arm through the material.

As if reacting to her words, Matthew threw his gaze to the ceiling. He was worried about giving the truth away through his expression alone. He shrugged. "I mean, I can't say I know what you see," he answered. "Maybe we've spent too much time together."

Ophelia chuckled softly. "Maybe," she conceded.

The severity of the conversation faded just as quickly as it had begun. Matthew levelled his head to look at Ophelia once again. Guilt ate at him like a parasite as he watched her. Such a strong and determined woman, her life torn to pieces because of him. If she had had her affair with anyone but him... things wouldn't be this way. Or, at the very least, she'd have a man to possibly run away with. All she wanted was to find Samuel. And she would never get that.

There was a sudden knock on the door before either of them could say anything else.

"Come in," Ophelia called.

Matthew was surprised when the door opened to reveal Titus in the doorway. He was even more surprised when Ophelia stood up as if she were expecting him.

"I've got to go now," she told Matthew. She must have seen the confusion plastered over the shifter's face because she elaborated. "Titus and I pray together each afternoon."

Normally, Matthew would have scoffed. He had personally never seen the use of praying to a being that may or may not exist. At this moment, he was glad for Titus' ability to bring some comfort to Ophelia. He knew that religion often provided a hope that many couldn't conjure in themselves. Just because he didn't believe in the practice himself didn't mean that he didn't respect other people's right to practice it. The only time he took issue with it was when Titus would preach at him about his actions and the consequences they would have in the eyes of God.

"It was nice speaking to you, Matthew," Ophelia said.

"You too, Ophelia," Matthew smiled.

"Look after that letter," she reminded him.

Matthew nodded. "I will, I promise."

Once Ophelia had gone with Titus and the room was empty, Matthew opened Ophelia's letter.

Samuel,

I don't know if this letter will ever reach you. I have entrusted it to the hands of your brother, Matthew, in case you both ever cross paths again.

I understand why you did what you did. Our arrangement wasn't supposed to last. I understand why you gave the hotel a different address. For all you knew, I could have followed you home or come to your house at ridiculous hours simply to pester you for more attention. I would have done the same if I had been put in a similar position. For a moment, when we were together, I was able to forget the brutality that waited for me in reality. You gave me a moment of respite; of relief; of freedom; and I only wish I had gotten a chance to thank you for that before you disappeared. So, I wish to thank you now. Thank you, Samuel.

I can only hope now that you stay away. My husband wishes us both dead, but that doesn't mean that he must succeed. Please, Samuel, wherever you are, don't ever return. This is my own doing, and I will face the consequences alone. Maybe this is God's way of punishing me for my infidelity. Either way, it is my cross to bear.

I wish you a happy, healthy life far from me and the burden of my tyrant of a husband. I hope I was able to provide you with the same reprieve that you gave me. Even if it was only momentary, it would then feel like it had been worth it all.

Yours sincerely,

Ophelia

Matthew covered his face with his hands and bit back tears. He wished he could tell Ophelia that she had given him the same respite; relief; reprieve and freedom. But most of all, he wished he could tell her that he wished that they had never met. That way, she would be safe.

Safe from him and his curse.

CHAPTER SEVEN

"So, while you lot were here doing nothing, I did some digging around."

Six sets of unamused eyes met Thursday at the end of her statement. She had called them all together for an important meeting. Well, he called, she just yelled around the house for everyone to join her in the dining room until they did. Matthew didn't know what she could possibly have to say, but she claimed it was concerning Ophelia's situation.

Not seeming to notice the glares of her peers, Thursday reached into her bag and threw a bunch of pages out onto the table. Sybil was immediately reaching across and gathering them all together to read.

"It wasn't hard to get information on Ophelia's husband. Once she gave a name, all I had to do was ask around a bit. I even entered the police station itself and asked a couple of officers about him," she explained.

"And?" Whitney prompted. "Find anything worthwhile?"

Thursday nodded in the direction of the papers in Sybil's hands. "Charles Davenport. Sorry, I should say *Commissioner* Charles Davenport. Luckily, he wasn't around when I popped in today, but I got the general impression from the force that he is well-rounded; mentally stable; and a perfectly decent man."

"Do you believe them?" Matthew asked.

Thursday put her hands on her hips. "The force is obviously biased. They have been working with Charles since who knows when. I didn't even bring up Ophelia because I believe they could be aware of Charles' intentions for her."

"She did say that Charles had connections in the force who would be willing to help him," Sybil murmured from somewhere behind the papers Thursday had gathered.

"What about the people outside of the force?" Titus was leaning toward Sybil, examining the information on the pages over her shoulder. "What did they have to say?"

Thursday's face melted into a smirk. "They had a completely different impression of dear Commissioner Charles."

"Oh? In what way?"

"Charles is rumoured to be a wife beater and a predator. Ophelia has been known to be spotted with bruises on her face and hands. When asked she had always claimed she had walked into doors or tripped, of course. Their neighbours have made their displeasure at the noise they make at night clear. So much so that everyone who knows the pair of them is aware of their domestic… issues. She disappeared about a month ago, having had enough of him. The whole 'my husband is coming home' act was probably just for Samuel."

It fit Ophelia's profile, especially after having read her letter the previous day. Matthew sunk into his seat and tried to keep his face indifferent. He felt horrible about never making Samuel question Ophelia on why she had wanted to escape her husband. There had to have been something he could have done. If only he had had the sense to ask Ophelia why a married woman had wished to have an affair.

"I have a feeling that even if Ophelia had claimed that Charles had hit her, he would use his standing in the police to escape charge," Whitney mused.

"Most likely, yes," Thursday agreed. "Which is probably why she chose to lie instead."

"I didn't notice any bodily damage when we were"- Matthew stopped dead in his tracks. It felt odd talking about what he had done with Ophelia in front of everyone. He didn't know if it was because of a newfound reservation about discussing his private life or if it had something to do with the fact that there was now a new member of their group who was currently watching him with annoyingly captivating blue eyes.

"Not all abuse is physical," Whitney replied. She hugged herself and shook her head. "Who knows how else he manipulates her? Sometimes, words can have just as much of an effect on us."

"Manipulation is torture on the same level as the asylum's therapy," Thursday nodded. She paused before amending, "The asylum's therapy *was* manipulation. They try to mould us into creatures of their will."

"It's also extremely common amongst narcissists," Finn added. "And narcissism is a key element in the psyche of an abuser."

Matthew was surprised when the healer spoke. Since it was his first official meeting with the rest of the group, Matthew had expected Finn to remain silent and absorb everything. It was what Matthew himself had done at his first group meeting. He had been scared to speak up out of fear of saying something wrong. He didn't know what the rules were and-okay-Thursday had intimidated him slightly in the beginning (but he would never tell her that).

"Narcissism?" there was confusion in Titus' voice. Thursday looked quite lost also.

"Vanity; self-absorbed; full of oneself," Sybil clarified.

"Oh, so basically Matthew?" This was the first time Sawyer had spoken during the entire meeting.

Matthew rolled his eyes and ignored Sawyer. Since Sawyer was not interested in helping Ophelia in the slightest, he had not been expected to participate. If he were to say anything, it was not going to be helpful to their current task.

"If you don't have anything useful to say, Sawyer, please refrain from speaking," Sybil stated blandly, not even looking at her partner as she spoke.

"Sorry," Titus quickly said to Finn, somewhat sheepish, "I've been catching up on my missed education, but it takes time."

Finn smiled warmly. "Don't apologise for that. I didn't have an official education, either. I'm self-taught."

Matthew found himself staring at Finn. It was like the healer was a beacon of light and Matthew was a moth trapped in the dark. Finn's presence demanded Matthew's attention as much as Ophelia's had done. And not through a dominating demeanour or forceful sense of self. It wasn't even about how he looked or dressed.

There was just something in the way he sat a couple of seats down, across the table from Matthew, one hand gently laid on the dark wood while the other rested comfortably on top of his cane. About how he participated despite having not been part of a group meeting before. About how he had taken the situation with Ophelia into his stride and didn't question why they wished to help her. About how he didn't even question Matthew's involvement with her.

Everything about his behaviour was mesmerizing. Everything about his actions turned Matthew's head back to him, in wait for what he was going to do or say next.

"Did you get any information on his recent whereabouts?" Sybil enquired.

Thursday shook her head. "I couldn't," she admitted. "The people who don't work with him say that they haven't seen him in a while. According to the force, he is taking some time off, but who knows if they are telling the truth or not."

"How long has it been since he was seen?" Matthew asked.

"A week?" Whitney guessed.

Thursday nodded. "Yeah. A week."

"So, basically, since Ophelia arrived at our house. Which we can only assume means since he discovered that she had slept with Matthew." Sybil's eyebrows creased. "Samuel, I mean." She looked up from the table. "This was some really good work, Thursday."

"I didn't think you cared so much," Whitney muttered.

The madwoman shrugged. "Just helping a friend out of a jam." Her eyes caught Matthew's and she grinned. Matthew smiled back, warmth spreading throughout him at the support of his friend.

"You're no closer, you know," Sawyer elected to remind them. "You have no idea where he is."

"I'm sorry, I don't recall asking you to speak, Sawyer," Thursday said sweetly.

This made Sawyer chuckle. "Don't you see? This is pointless. We'll never find this Charles man. He has too much power behind him anyway, especially if he has the police force on his side. I vote we just kick this Ophelia woman out of the house and let fate have its way." The way his mouth curled into a smirk at this, Matthew knew that he didn't mean fate as in the natural order of things.

Sybil slammed Thursday's papers down onto the table. "Sawyer, if you *dare*"-

"*Relax*, I don't care enough," Sawyer interrupted. "I've never been able to bring myself to care about humans unless they benefit me in some way, which they rarely do. This entire escapade is just an entire waste of your time."

An image of Ophelia thrust out into the streets to fend for herself flashed through Matthew's mind. He flushed angrily and stood up. "Protecting someone's life is not a waste of our time!"

Sawyer didn't so much as flinch at Matthew's outburst. He lazily cast his eyes over the shifter critically before rolling them to make his boredom clear. "Evolution will eventually take care of them, what does it matter if we speed up the process for some?"

"Evolution?" Matthew exclaimed incredulously. "What on earth are you talking about?"

"It's basic science," Sawyer sighed, waving his hand dismissively. "The theory of evolution. The seven of us are ahead of everybody else. Someday the world will be empty of the primates and there will be more of us."

"Who cares about science?" Matthew snapped. "This is about using our abilities for something decent besides lounging around this mansion. Isn't that what we should be heading for? Using our advancements to help people rather than cowering in the dark? What is the point of training ourselves if we aren't willing to put the training to use?"

Sawyer pulled a face. "They won't accept us, you know. If they knew what we could do, there would be a witch hunt."

An unwelcome image burst into Matthew's mind of the children he had lived with in the orphanage. How he had been dubbed a freak because he had no way of controlling his ability. They accused him of practising witchcraft; of using magic; of being the spawn of Satan sent to tempt them. He knew that he had been days away from being cast out before Thursday found him.

That didn't mean he wished them dead. They just didn't understand.

"I will not let Charles kill Ophelia," Matthew said firmly, his voice practically trembling with emotion.

Sawyer's dark eyes bored into him, a smug look on his face. "You're only saying that because you changed shape and had her like some sort of whor"-

"Sawyer!" Sybil shouted.

Sawyer's gaze didn't shift from Matthew. They glared at each other, nothing but hatred and spite in one another's eyes. Matthew didn't know if he could portray every ill feeling he had towards Sawyer through a stare alone, but he was willing to try. His chest was rising and falling because of how angry he felt. This feeling was only made worse by how calm Sawyer seemed. How could he be so hateful and remain so placid?

"I've got to go," Whitney suddenly said. Her voice broke Matthew's stare as he turned to watch her stumble to her feet. Her face was flushed bright pink, and she was clutching her hands to her chest. Her skin was beginning to glow like the embers of a fire were sparking from her skin. Her eyebrows were also scrunched together, a clear look of contempt on her face.

Matthew watched her flee the room wordlessly.

Sybil thrust her own chair back angrily and glared at both Matthew and Sawyer. "Have some consideration for the emotions of the people around you before you start another shouting match," she snarled.

Without saying anything else, she hurried after Whitney.

There was a long, drawn-out silence where no one dared speak.

"Let's hope she doesn't blow a hole in the house," Sawyer eventually said. He slung himself to his feet, a casual smile on his face as he too strode out of the room.

"You're such a ratbag sometimes," Thursday threw at his back.

"I know, it's wonderful, isn't it?" Sawyer called back just as the door shut behind him.

Thursday spun on her heel and left through the opposite door, clearly irritated by her lack of ability to get under Sawyer's skin. Matthew thought she would have figured this out after his shouting match with said ratbag, but then Thursday was more of a doer than an observer. She had to do it for herself just to make sure it was impossible.

Obviously uncomfortable, Titus was the next to take leave. "Ophelia will be waiting for me to say prayers," he muttered, more to himself than to Matthew.

Matthew fell back into his seat pathetically, feeling defeated. Nothing he said or did was ever good enough. Even when it was something he genuinely believed in, like the protection of Ophelia, he still couldn't seem to get anything right. He felt awful for getting Whitney angry when she was in such a vulnerable position with her emotions. He took comfort in the fact that Sawyer was making her more annoyed than he was, but that didn't mean he couldn't have stopped yelling before the argument got too frustrating for her to handle.

"I agree with you."

Matthew looked up from the table to Finn. "Oh? About what?"

Finn gave a one-armed shrug. "About our abilities. Or gifts. Or however what is wrong with us is viewed. We can't just sit on top of them and do nothing. We need to do something with them. Help people; save them… Heal them."

Matthew smiled wearily. "You said you wanted to be a doctor," he reminded him.

This made the healer raise his eyebrows. "Does that somehow prevent me from helping people? Is it not a doctor's purpose to help people?"

Matthew hadn't considered that. "At least someone agrees with me," he muttered.

"I wouldn't say the others don't. From what I could see, the only person who didn't share your viewpoint was Sawyer. His views on humans are… unique."

"Mad, more like," Matthew responded. He stood up again and waved his hands helplessly. "Imagine knowing someone's death was your fault and being okay with that? I wouldn't be able to sleep at night."

"That's completely normal," said Finn. "I believe that's how most people think."

Matthew pushed his hand through his hair. "Yes, well, I suppose Sawyer has always been different from everyone else. Not in a good way, might I add."

Finn slowly nodded his agreement. He suddenly looked thoughtful. "His eye. Was he born with it looking that way?"

This question made Matthew pull a face. "Yes. Why?"

"Another genetic anomaly," Finn mused.

There was a part of Matthew that was annoyed. He didn't want Finn to consider Sawyer's birthmark another interesting genetic anomaly. It was selfish of him, but he wanted the praise of being unique and exclusive to him. He wanted to be the only one Finn found interesting or special in any way.

"I like yours better," Finn concluded. As if realising a moment later what he had said, Finn blushed and added, "I mean, yours is more striking. His is very... uncomfortable."

Matthew felt his rage at Sawyer melt away at Finn's compliment. A smile twitched onto his face. "You think so?"

"Of course," Finn replied, more apprehensive than before. "I'm sure Ophelia thought so too. Or do your eyes also change?"

"Everything changes," Matthew shrugged. "What you see right now is a blank page that everyone else gets to fill in. Nobody wants an empty page."

Finn was wearing an expression Matthew couldn't decipher. "You seem to be insinuating that you are boring. Was it not yourself who told me you weren't a bore? Surely, you realise that someone with such strong vigour as yourself is far from boring."

Matthew winced. Not out of pain but disbelief. "The only people who get to experience the real me are the ones currently residing in this house. And one of them believes I'm the brother of one of my alters."

"That is very unfortunate," Finn said quietly.

Matthew didn't know whether the healer had intended for him to hear or not. He seemed to have been talking to himself.

"Do you intend to continue with Ophelia?" Finn enquired.

The question threw Matthew off. He wasn't sure where it had come from. "I can't," he said. "I wouldn't play with her emotions like that."

"So, you don't intend to turn back into Samuel and continue life with her?" Finn was looking at the table. Matthew didn't know if he was right or not, but he could have sworn there was concern in the healer's tone.

"No." Matthew had not realised that he had been moving around the table to Finn's side until he was standing right beside the healer's chair. He was so close he could reach out and touch the bronze strands of Finn's hair. His fingers twitched by his side at the thought. "Why?"

"Just curious." It was the first time Matthew had heard Finn stammer or sound at all nervous since he had come out of the infirmary.

Matthew fell into the seat beside Finn. He wished he had chosen to sit here for the entire meeting. Simply being in the healer's proximity soothed him. Like somehow not only did Finn's hands have healing properties but his whole existence did. Matthew was tempted to slide his seat closer just to feel it better.

It occurred to Matthew that he still hadn't pursued Finn in the way he had told Thursday he would. Even now, thinking about it made him grimace. The way he had worded it. *Get him into bed.* It sounded too cheap. Matthew didn't want to do that anymore. He had grown to respect Finn too much to treat him like he treated everyone else. He would have to figure Finn out the old-fashioned way. Or, at the very least, until a time came when he felt he had earned the right to such a private action.

"Sawyer reminds me of the people who ran the circus." Finn's voice was quiet again, but Matthew knew that he had intended for him to hear this time. "They only cared about themselves.

Never the people they considered below them. They weren't even worth sparing a thought about."

Matthew listened to Finn. He understood what he was saying but could not imagine what it felt like to be one of those people considered beneath someone else. It made his anger at Sawyer well up again. This was what happened when one side treated the other differently just because they were... well... different.

Finn had begun tracing a ridge on the top of his hand. Matthew immediately knew it was a whipping scar. "Despite it all, I would never wish a human to die. There have been many times when I've thought about it, sure, but I would never act upon it. I don't believe in condemning an entire species simply from the actions of a handful. Despite what they did to me. Despite what they did to others to make me heal them. They don't represent them all." A pause. "Does that make sense or am I just rambling?"

"It makes sense," Matthew said, his voice the same volume as Finn's. "We shouldn't become the monsters they expect us to be."

Finn turned his head to look at Matthew. His eyes were shining with admiration. Someone was looking at him with admiration. *Him.* Not contempt, or amusement, or mocking. Admiration. The sight warmed Matthew's soul.

Matthew reached across the small space between them and placed his hand on top of Finn's. He could feel the hard ridge of the scar pressed against his palm. It made his muscles tense with hatred. Here was a man who had suffered at the hands of human beings, yet still believed in their protection. Finn had more excuse to wish humans dead than Sawyer ever did or ever would. Yet, he turned a situation from something abhorrent into something beautiful. Finn had decided that he wanted to prevent suffering instead of causing it.

When Finn smiled at him, Matthew felt himself gravitate towards him. His being was on autopilot, riddled with nerves and anxiety. Never had he felt such fear at the prospect of kissing someone. Never had he had to worry about rejection until now.

Finn didn't move towards Matthew, but he didn't pull back either. They were so close that they were breathing onto one another's faces. Matthew's heart pounded but he couldn't lose his nerve now. Even if Finn pushed him away, at least he could say that he had tried.

Finn's eyes had just flickered shut and Matthew could feel the tremor in the healer's breathing when the door flung open. It banged against the opposite wall like a bomb exploding beside the table.

They both jumped apart.

Thursday slowed as she passed them. "Did I interrupt something?" she asked, quirking an eyebrow.

"No, no," Matthew and Finn both said at the same time.

Thursday didn't look convinced. Usually, Matthew would not have a problem telling Thursday about his actions, but he knew that Finn would not be as open. So, because he knew Finn would be embarrassed, Matthew didn't say anything. Not because he was afraid of overstepping a boundary, but because Matthew genuinely didn't want to do anything that would make Finn afraid or uncomfortable.

In times like these, so much as considering holding the hand of the same sex could be punishable by law. Matthew had had plenty of time to adjust to his desires to the point where he now had no fear. Finn, however, had only openly expressed his longings a week ago, and it hadn't been by his own free will. This was an extremely delicate situation, and Matthew didn't want to do something that could ruin everything. He wanted Finn to be comfortable in himself and his desires and to have the option to choose how he wished to proceed with it.

"Right," Thursday said slowly. She drifted across the room to the opposite door, a salacious smirk growing on her face with every step she took. "I'll see you kids later."

Once she was gone, Finn deflated. He put his face in his arms. Matthew watched him, unsure of what to say. He reached out and placed his hand on Finn's back. "It's okay," he said quietly.

"I'm so used to suppressing this," Finn answered into his arms.

Matthew's lips tightened. Part with anger, part with sympathy. He wasn't angry at Finn. He was angry at the state of the world that put him in this position. "I know," he replied. "You're safe here. There's nothing to worry about."

"It's easy to say, but when you've spent your entire life scared to even so much as glance at another man in case... they can read your mind and just... *know*... It's not so easy anymore."

Matthew could feel that Finn was shaking a bit with nerves. He didn't know whether it was trembling caused by their impending kiss or by Thursday walking in on them and their impending kiss. He didn't know what it felt like to have lived with such fear. He had lived in the orphanage for most of his life until Thursday found him. Once he settled into Sybil's mansion and discovered who he was, he was in a comforting and accepting environment.

"I appreciate that what you did was out of guilt, but it's unnecessary. I'm a mess. You don't want to even attempt to get involved," Finn explained.

"Guilt?" Matthew repeated, confused. Finn thought he tried to kiss him out of guilt. "I didn"-

Voices could suddenly be heard, coming closer and closer to the door Thursday had just left through. They burst open, Sawyer barging through with Sybil in close tow.

"I don't understand how you can be so cruel!" Sybil was yelling at Sawyer's back. "This isn't a trivial matter!"

"If telling it as it is will be considered cruel now then I guess I am," Sawyer barked. It seemed the only person who could get the madman to lose his cool was Sybil. Sybil had a specific kind of rage that not even he could ignore. "This human is nothing but a waste of our time and resources!"

"What resources? We have plenty of resources!" Sybil snapped. She lurched forward and grabbed Sawyer's arm to stop him from getting away from her. "Since when have you cared about resources, Sawyer?"

"Ever since this place became a boarding house to fil"-Sawyer stopped, noticing Matthew and Finn still seated at the table. As he did, Sybil also turned and noticed them.

"We didn't think anyone would still be here," Sybil muttered, releasing Sawyer's arm.

Sawyer immediately took off, not wasting any time getting away from Sybil.

Sybil didn't pursue Sawyer. Instead, she stood by the table, a fixed expression on her face. She was looking at Finn, who was still trembling with Matthew's hand on his back. "Everything okay?" she asked.

"Yes," Finn immediately answered. He quickly stood up and hobbled away.

Matthew watched Finn leave, the clicking of his cane hitting the floor heard long after he had disappeared from the room. He looked at his hand, the one that had sat on top of the healer's back. He chewed his lip. He could feel Sybil watching him.

"Is he telling the truth?" Sybil eventually asked.

It took Matthew a moment to process the question. He was still looking at his hand. His skin was beginning to tingle. "Yeah," he answered unconvincingly.

"Don't lie to me, Matthew. I don't like it," Sybil immediately responded.

Matthew finally lifted his eyes from his hand to look at his leader. She wasn't angry with him. Her face had concern etched into every inch of her skin. "It's between me and him," Matthew told her. "It's a private matter."

Sybil didn't look too pleased with his response, but she seemed to understand. She knew when to push and when to leave be. Matthew liked that about her.

"Okay," she said. "Just... remember that he's new to all of this."

Matthew nodded. "Don't worry, I do."

Sybil didn't follow Sawyer. Instead, she sighed and exited through the route they had entered through. This left Matthew alone at the table to contemplate what had just happened.

The reaction that he had gotten from Finn was standard. He had bedded people who weren't open about their sexuality before and knew how the very prospect could make them feel. A lot of them were confident in their hiding. If they knew someone was interested, then they had nothing to fear. Others never imagined they would ever be put into the position of being able to explore that part of themselves. So, when they're put into that position, they get scared and riddled with anxiety. Matthew guessed that Finn fell into the latter category.

Matthew was suddenly glad that he had put aside what he had told Thursday. It felt cheap. He only wished that Thursday hadn't interrupted them just now. He wished he had gotten to taste the healer's lips, even if it had only been for a moment.

Still, he wasn't going to push Finn into anything he wasn't comfortable with. He wasn't even going to press that it was nothing to fear so that Finn would let him try anything like he usually did with nervous people.

Matthew wanted Finn to want him back. Not with carnal greed; dirty longing; or desperate lust. He wanted Finn to yearn for his company the same way Matthew had grown to yearn for Finn's. It was a foreign feeling, one that Matthew had never experienced before. He was so used to wanting people to crave him in the way that he craved them. He had never wanted emotions. Emotions only led to complications.

In a way, Matthew wanted to be complicated with Finn.

Did that even make sense?

Matthew rubbed a hand over his face and groaned to himself.

Why was everything so difficult? Why was Finn making everything so complex? He was just one man. Matthew had met many men before, what made this one so different?

You didn't change for him.

It had been a while since Matthew had thought about that.

What did that mean? Was it possible that his ability had malfunctioned for a moment and his body didn't shift for Finn? That didn't add up. If it had simply been a malfunction, then surely Matthew would have shifted the next time he saw Finn. But he hadn't.

Could Thursday be right? Could Finn's idea of perfect beauty be exactly as Matthew was? How could that be? There was no way that Finn had imagined exactly how Matthew looked before he had even met him. Surely, something should have changed. Even if Matthew's hair had changed colour, then it would make much more sense. However, *nothing* changed. Nothing at all.

It wasn't like there was some sort of rule book Matthew could refer himself to so he could get the answers that he wanted. There was no shifter guidebook written by shifter ancestors. There was only him. Matthew. He'd end up writing the guidebook. Great. How was he going to write about something he had no clue about?

Matthew huffed and stood up, finally deciding to leave the room. There was no point sitting alone in the dining room staring at the wall like some sort of dazed lunatic. He had been getting lost in his thoughts a lot recently. Something else that had been brought about by Finn's appearance. Matthew was far from an intellectual. He had never been a big thinker. Yet, ever since Finn had come into his life, his brain had been alive with tangled thoughts that he needed to straighten out.

Never had Matthew thought that finding Friday would do this to him.

Was all this wondering pointless? For all he knew, he could be pining over someone who would never see him as anything more than a friend. Matthew knew he could be setting himself up for severe emotional damage. It was why he never let himself express any emotion for another human beyond comradery or lust. Matthew felt like he was holding his heart in his hand, waiting for the right moment to extend his arm to let Finn stab it.

Matthew paused in the doorway as he suddenly thought of something.

Finn had closed his eyes.

Before Thursday came in, Finn had not moved away as Matthew had drawn closer, and as their faces were inches apart, he had closed in eyes. Had he been about to accept the kiss? Could it be possible that Finn was just as confused about Matthew as Matthew was confused about Finn?

Matthew shook his head. There were more important things to be focusing on. Keeping Ophelia alive was his priority.

Besides, it was probably only wishful thinking to hope that someone like Finn would want someone like him.

CHAPTER EIGHT

MATTHEW JERKED AWAKE. What was that noise?

He looked at the clock by his bedside. Two in the morning. Typical.

With an aggravated sigh, Matthew lit his bedside lamp on and threw his covers back. If this was Thursday running around the halls again, he was going to consider getting a lock for her bedroom door. These early morning escapades were entertaining to only Thursday. Since his bedroom was right beside hers, there was some sort of unspoken rule that Matthew was responsible for reeling her in in the middle of the night.

He poked his head out the door. "Thursday?" he whispered.

There was no response. Usually, at this point, Thursday would have come dancing out of the shadows, most likely drunk, and tried to drag him off into some sort of indoor adventure with her.

This time, there was nothing.

The hallway was eerily silent. Everything was shrouded in thick darkness, not a single lamp lit.

The sound that had woke him up, however, was much clearer. Matthew stepped out into the hallway to listen better. It was footsteps of some kind, that's why he had assumed it was Thursday. Now that he was out of his room, he could tell that the sound was coming from below him, not on the same floor.

Just to confirm his suspicions, Matthew moved to Thursday's door and pressed his ear against it. He could just about make out her breathing on the other side of the wood.

Then who was wandering around downstairs?

Matthew peered over the bannister. He squinted, trying to make out the floors below him through the darkness. The light from the small flame in his lamp didn't extend far enough down for him to see more than a few paces in front of him.

As his eyes were adjusting, he began to make out tiny black blobs a couple of floors down. They were stopping, by what he could tell, at each door. Opening them up. Peering in. Moving on.

Intruders.

Matthew's heart picked up. Sybil's house wasn't a stranger to thieves. Its extravagance was practically a siren call to lawbreakers. There wasn't any time to wake any of the others up. Doing so would only alert the intruders to the fact they had been discovered. So, with no choice, Matthew decided he had to act alone.

He tiptoed along the hallway and slid down the stairs as quietly as he could. As he reached the same floor as the assumed thieves, he slinked closer without drawing their attention. He hung back in the shadows, waiting for the right moment to act.

"Not that one either?" one of the invaders whispered.

"No," another hissed back. "How big is this bloody house?"

"So many rooms," a different one said. "How are we going to find her here?"

The group moved down to the next door. Matthew followed, his heart in his throat as he listened to their conversation. Who were they looking for? It couldn't possibly be… Ophelia, could it? Impossible. How could Charles have found her so fast?

Two disappeared into the next room, while one remained stationed outside.

Matthew saw his opening. He reached out to the closest lamp and turned the gas on, plunging the small space around it into a yellow glow as the flame flickered on.

This immediately caught the attention of the person stationed outside the room. Matthew noted that it was a middle-aged male who was quite tall and well-built. The flame from the lamp illuminated the startled expression on their face as they jerked their head in the direction of the light.

Matthew shuddered as the man's eyes hit him. The change sometimes felt like a seizure. It was so sudden and violent. He felt hair brush his arms and back and the ground almost seemed to eat him as he shrank a couple of inches. Taking this in his stride, he smiled and waved at the man, whose startled expression had now changed to one of reverence.

Matthew flicked his head, indicating for the man to come closer. Of course, he did. He drifted towards Matthew like he was on autopilot. As he reached the pool of light provided by the lamp, Matthew was able to make out a litter of orange freckles across his nose and cheeks.

"You're…" the man trailed off, his lips parting in wonderment.

Matthew curled his finger under the man's chin. Thinking that this was an extension of intimacy, the man slid closer, reaching for Matthew's face with wide eyes and shaking hands. The change usually caused this type of reaction. It was too much for the brain to comprehend. An image was confronting the system that it thought it had only conjured with its imagination. That must have had some sort of impact on the body.

Their faces were so close now that Matthew could smell the alcohol and cigarettes on the other man's breath. Rolling his eyes, Matthew grabbed the man's hair and smashed his head off the wall. He winced at the sound of the intruder's skull cracking against the hard brick of the wall, and he released him to let his body flop to the floor.

Another man rushed out of the room at the sound of Matthew's attack, and Matthew knew that he only had a couple of seconds to get this guy before the other one followed.

Matthew stepped over the first man's body and held his thin arms out. "Come on, then!" he shouted, grabbing the attention of the new man. "I'm right here!"

This man took a run up at him, but the instant his eyes hit Matthew and Matthew changed for him, he staggered to a stop. Not having a lot of time, Matthew used the man's short pause to rush him. He tackled him full force, bringing them both to the floor.

He was still in the form of a woman, a quite frail one at that, so punching was out of the question. Matthew's main attack wasn't punching or kicking out anyway: it was always instinct for him to go for the head. It was most likely because he was used to fighting in the forms of the thin; small; frail women formed in the heads of egotistical males.

Matthew smashed this man's head against the floor three times. He was seeing red, about to go for a fourth when a fresh shudder hit him. It threw him off guard and he paused, heart thundering in his chest. It was only for a moment, but that was enough.

Two arms wound around his waist and lifted him off the now unconscious man like he was nothing but a bag of spuds.

He was thrown against the bannister and held there. A malevolent face loomed over him in the faint glow from the lamp. It wasn't an ugly face. Matthew had always expected thieves and criminals to be disgusting creatures with missing teeth and dirty hair. This man looked normal.

"I found you," the man growled.

What? Who? Found who?

"Did you think you could hide from me?" he snarled. "I told you I'd always find you!"

A hand curled around Matthew's throat and squeezed. His hands flew to the ones around his neck, trying to pry the iron-clad grip open. He choked, eyes staring wide at his attacker in disbelief. Who did this man think he was?

That was when he noticed what his new hands looked like.

They were pale. Like porcelain. Like... snow.

Had he turned into Ophelia?

"Charles!"

Ophelia stood at the end of the hallway now, her chest heaving like she had run a mile. She looked dishevelled, probably having just jumped out of bed. Her face was twisted with horror and fear, but the emotion that dominated them all was rage.

"Charles, let him go!" she screamed. "This is between you and me!"

"How did you get there?" Charles shouted back at her. He looked down at Matthew, who had used the opportunity to flicker back to normal. His confusion made his fingers tighten around the shifter's throat, rather than loosen. "What sort of sorcery is this?"

"This isn't Matthew's fight!" Ophelia yelled. "Let him go!"

Charles growled and glared down at Matthew. "Are you her new man? The next one she's chosen to betray me through. Better than the Spic, but she has learned nothing."

Matthew felt like he was staring into the face of evil. He couldn't find a single glimmer of remorse or resentment in Charles' eyes. Even now as he stood strangling a man, one he did not know at all, there was nothing but fury behind his gaze. In a way, it reminded Matthew of Sawyer.

This revelation ignited a fire inside Matthew. He was not going to be bettered by a being of hatred and emptiness.

Matthew drew his fist back and punched the smug smirk straight off Charles' face. It was enough to get the human to loosen his grip on his throat and stumble back a step. Matthew flexed his jaw, ignoring the burning sensation at the bottom of his back from being thrown against the bannister. Charles held fast to this neck, holding for grim death despite being knocked for six.

"Matthew, don't!" Ophelia shouted. "This is *my* fight! He'll kill you!"

"I'd like to see him try," Matthew growled.

At the end of his sentence, there was a thunderous crash from above. Matthew looked up as Thursday came barging out of her room, face twisted with wrath. "I'm trying to sleep!" she roared as she leapt over the bannister and fell past them.

Ophelia screamed in shock, flying to the bannister on her current floor to see where Thursday had landed. Matthew knew there wouldn't be a sound of her hitting the floor, nor would there be a body crumpled in the foyer. Thursday wasn't the sudden suicide sort. Certainly not over something as trivial as being woken up in the middle of the night.

There was an explosion of purple and Thursday flew back up towards them, leaping over Ophelia's horrified head. She ignored the stunned woman as she focused her attention on Charles.

"I don't know you," she snarled. "But you don't have long to release him before I make you."

"How many people did you hire for your protection, Ophelia?" Charles snapped. He looked straight past Thursday like she wasn't even a threat to him.

"Do I look like a woman who works for hire?" Thursday looked disgusted at the very idea.

Charles' fingers tightened around Matthew's throat. Matthew tried to exhale but Charles' grip wouldn't allow it. He gagged, the sound drawing Charles' attention back to the fact that he was, in fact, currently strangling someone.

"Stay out of my affairs if you know what's good for you," he said to Thursday, returning his focus to Matthew, "*woman.*"

"Woman?" Thursday repeated.

If Matthew could breathe correctly, he would have laughed at Charles. He had just hammered the final nail into his coffin. A man who used the gender of a person to insult someone was no man at all. However, the fact that he had directed this insult at Thursday just made the situation shift from rude to perilous.

Charles had turned from Thursday, an evil look in his eyes as he put all his attention back into strangling Matthew. Matthew choked, his vision beginning to black around the edges. A distinct purple began to line this blackness, and soon Charles wasn't looking at Matthew again. Then he had dropped him to the ground.

Matthew gasped, his throat throbbing with every beat of his heart. From behind him, Charles was yelling.

"What sort of she-demon are you?" he barked.

"*She-demon.* I like that," Thursday replied.

Matthew rolled onto his back just in time to catch Thursday send a blast of her 'glow,' as she called it, at the wall by Charles' head. The impact shook the lamps lining the hallway, the doorknobs rattling like cutlery in a drawer.

"How did you find this house?" Thursday barked at Charles.

Charles foolishly did not want to appear afraid of a woman but from where Matthew lay, he could see the man's fists trembling. "My men followed you. Did you honestly think you wouldn't be followed when you came into the station recklessly asking questions about me? You were obviously in league with the whore."

"Her name is Ophelia," Matthew gasped, still not having gotten his breath completely back. He kicked his leg out and tripped Charles up.

Charles landed heavily on top of the first man Matthew had killed. He hardly seemed to care as his eyes flew between Matthew and Thursday. He eventually looked past them both and stared at Ophelia. "What is this?" he demanded. "Have you pledged allegiance with Satanists in exchange for protection?"

Thursday burst out laughing. "Wait until Titus hears that one!" she cackled.

"These people are not Satanists." Ophelia's voice shook as she stepped up beside Thursday. "They are... friends."

"What? A man who changes his face and a woman with the fires of hell coming from her very hands?" Charles screamed back at her. His face had gone red and twisted. "Nothing can explain this besides black magic and Satan's work!"

Footsteps came thundering down from somewhere above them.

Sybil appeared moments later, her hair wild and tangled as she flew down the steps to join them in the hallway. "I heard a blast!" she shouted. Her eyebrows were furrowed. She was getting ready to scold whoever was responsible for the ruckus. Then she took in the situation. "What…?"

"Charles was nice enough to hand himself over to us," Thursday beamed, gesturing to the man on the floor.

Charles looked over his shoulder at Sybil and tutted. He had intended for it to be to himself, but Sybil had never been one to miss quiet utterances. She had argued with enough of the group to learn how to hear such things.

Sybil walked closer until she stood over Charles' shoulder. "Come with me, Charles, I have a lovely room in the basement that is perfect for you." She turned and headed back to the stairs as if expecting him to follow.

"Are you insane?" Charles spat at her.

Sybil looked over her shoulder at him and sighed. Without answering him, she flicked her hand out behind her. Charles' ankle immediately flew into the air, causing his back to hit the floor. The human man immediately began spouting obscenities, but it had no effect. Sybil continued her journey to the stairs, only this time Charles was dragged along behind her like an invisible hand was pulling him along.

Thursday skipped along behind them, looping her arm through Ophelia's, and forcing her to come along with her. It looked like some sort of insane funeral procession.

Matthew knew where Sybil was taking Charles. She was going to leave him in the empty cellar until morning when she could call an official meeting, and they could discuss their next move.

He realised that he was now sitting alone in the hallway with two dead bodies, chest heaving like he had run a thousand miles and throat constricting like he had tied a noose around himself. Matthew tried to touch his throat and immediately winced, hissing in pain, and moving his hand away. Charles had a strong grip.

He had nearly killed him.

He had been trying to do that, moron.

Matthew's breathing sped up. The realisation that he could have died just now seized hold of his being, stealing what little air he had in his lungs.

The hallway started spinning beneath him and he had to lie down. Still, the floor persisted in moving. Round, round, and round.

Matthew had never faced death before. He always figured that he wouldn't be afraid, that dying was going to be just like living. It just happened. Titus always spouted stuff about God's plan for everyone and how everyone had their time already set out for them. Matthew didn't believe in God, but he took comfort, in a way, in the idea that his death was already planned. He liked to imagine it was far, far, far in the future.

It had taken for him to be strangled to the edge of his existence to realise that there were things that he wanted to do with his sorry life. Things he wouldn't get to do if he died right here in the hallway. How had he never thought of such a thing before?

"Matthew?"

Whitney's face hovering above his. Someone moving him.

Up.

Up.

Up.

A knock on the door.

Cobalt blue.

Darkness.

CHAPTER NINE

HUMMING.

Who was humming?

Matthew couldn't find it in him to move. He felt completely content where he was. Everything around him was quiet and serene. He wasn't even bothered by the humming. It was like he was lying on a cloud, far removed from the rest of civilisation, tucked up in a blanket, safe from harm.

The longer he lay there, the clearer the humming grew to be. It faded into his consciousness gradually, like his ears were slowly growing to work again. The humming didn't make Matthew feel nervous, uncomfortable, or worried in any way. He felt comforted by it. There was something about the tune, or the tone of the song, or even the voice humming it, that made him feel content. Forgotten was the fear of Charles; or the tight grip that his fingers had had around his throat; or the panic he had felt as air refused to go into his lungs. It had been replaced by a sensation that resembled security. Safety. Protection.

As his ears continued to clear, it soon became apparent that it wasn't just humming, there were words attached as well.

Matthew forced his heavy eyes open.

It took a moment for his vision to adjust. Sunlight streamed in through a window in the ceiling, giving the room that he was in an almost nebulous golden glow. Dust particles floated in the beams of light like tiny insects, lazily drifting around with no destination. There was a soft pitter-patter sound coming from somewhere, but Matthew couldn't place what it was in his tired state.

Matthew looked down and realised there was a hand around his neck. His heart stuttered, memories of the previous night bursting into his mind once more. This hand wasn't squeezing him, though. Matthew still felt calm and comfortable. He felt safe.

"You're awake," a gentle voice said.

Matthew's eyes flickered up.

Bathed in sunshine, Finn smiled down at him. His hair was untamed, like a lion's mane around his head. There were bags under his eyes, but all Matthew could see was the shining blue iris,' filled with warmth.

Subconsciously, Matthew's hand slid up and laid on top of the hand around his neck. He knew what it was now. What the source of this overwhelming sense of peace and serenity was. Why he felt so safe, even though he had no idea where he was or what happened? Why there was a pitter-pattering all around him, despite the sunlight streaming in through the window.

He was being healed.

The light wasn't from the sun. It was raining outside. The heavenly golden glow was coming from Finn's hand. The hand around Matthew's neck. The hand that had removed the pain from Charles' murder attempt and replaced it with contentment. His head was in Finn's lap, and the healer had a hand resting on top of his neck, healing away the damage Charles had caused.

It felt too good to be true. Maybe he did die and all of Titus' preaching had meant something after all. Without exaggeration, Matthew felt like he was in heaven.

"You were singing," was the first thing he found himself saying. There wasn't a single crack to his voice. It was clear as day.

Finn's face turned red. "I... yeah," he said peevishly.

"I don't know the song."

"You wouldn't. My mother wrote it." Finn brushed his fingertips across Matthew's forehead, and he smiled. Matthew had to forcibly prevent his eyes from fluttering at how good the healer's touch felt on his skin. "How are you feeling?"

"Am I alive?" Matthew asked.

Finn chuckled. "Of course. What made you think you weren't?"

"I was strangled and the next thing I know I'm waking up here. All I can see is a celestial golden light and the face of an angel is staring down at me," Matthew answered. "Wouldn't you think the same?"

Finn's blush intensified. "You have just woken up from death's door and your response is to attempt… flirtation?"

Matthew grinned. "It's in my nature." He noticed that he hadn't let go of Finn's hand yet. This knowledge did not make him any more inclined to do so. "Where am I?"

"My room. Whitney brought you here last night," Finn explained. "You were having a panic attack and with the state that your throat was in, you were hyperventilating dangerously. You passed out shortly after she brought you up. She was very worried about you."

It surprised Matthew that it had been Whitney who had brought him to Finn. Thursday blasting the wall must have woken her up also, but she could have easily disappeared to search for Sybil instead of running straight into the danger. Matthew had always figured that she didn't like him much.

Well, he figured that she didn't like anyone much. He was taken aback by the knowledge that she had carried him up to the attic because she was worried about him.

"Where is she now?" Matthew asked.

"I sent her to bed. She was exhausted," Finn explained. "Her skin was frosting over from watching me heal you." He brushed his rusty hair out of his eyes. "Sybil came by this morning. There's to be a meeting this evening if you get any better. She filled me in on everything that happened."

Matthew was distracted. Ever since Finn had said the word 'bed,' the shifter had not been able to take his eyes off the bags weighing down Finn's lids.

Without thinking, he reached up and touched the healer's face. Finn flinched but didn't move away. "Have you slept since Whitney brought me up?"

"My ability works best if I am awake."

"That's not what I asked."

"But it is what I answered."

The corner of Matthew's mouth twitched, threatening to turn up into a smile. Finn was just as stubborn as he was. "You have to sleep."

"And I shall. Once I know you're healed."

Matthew gently prised Finn's hand from his throat. The golden glow faded a little, but not completely. "I am healed.

I feel like I could sing opera, my throat feels that good. Who knows, maybe you mended some vocal cords, too."

Finn rolled his eyes. "I can't work miracles," he teased. His expression turned stern. "In all seriousness, Matthew, are you truly okay? That man… he tried to kill you. Or at least that's what Sybil told me. Why?"

The concern in Finn's tone was one that Matthew wasn't used to. He knew that there were people who cared about him; he was far from a loveless being. However, no one ever outwardly expressed it, with Sybil as a maternal exception. The people under Sybil's roof were all reserved; forced to be so as a lesson from their pasts. No one who lived here had had an easy life up until this point, and it certainly affected how they expressed feelings towards each other. Thursday in particular chose to let her actions speak for her instead of allowing emotions to show. She wasn't the type of person who would let worry or fear for another show on her face.

Matthew was accustomed to this way of living. He understood why it had to be that way. It had taken him a long time to open himself to other people but that didn't mean that everyone else-who had much harder and darker histories than him-would do so as quickly.

"When Charles looked at me, I must have turned into Ophelia," Matthew answered, trying to shrug it off.

Finn closed his eyes and exhaled. "Yeah, that would do it," he said. "So, he was truly trying to kill you. Or her. You as her."

"Ophelia must have heard the noise because she came out and confronted him," Matthew explained. "But this only caused confusion and even though I was able to change back into my normal shape, Charles still seemed intent on killing me. I don't think he has the best of tempers."

Finn rubbed his hand over his face. "It is a relief that Thursday came when she did, then."

"Yes, she has a habit of showing up last minute. I could have used her sometime before the hands went around my throat."

Matthew smiled but it quickly faded when he saw how ashen Finn suddenly looked. He heaved himself out of his lap to sit at the edge of the bed. The healer looked disconcerted as if he had just escaped an awkward confrontation. He was staring at his hands, which sat limp in his lap.

"What's wrong?" Matthew asked.

"He really would have killed you," Finn said, speaking to his hands. "He could have *actually* killed you. You could have died last night."

"But, hey, I didn't," Matthew replied. "I'm alive."

Finn's eyes were wide, slowly tracing up and down the scar on his hand. Matthew watched him for a moment, confused by why this possibility seemed to have frightened Finn so.

Matthew took Finn's scarred hand and put it on his chest, over his heart. "See? Still battering away."

Finn continued to stare intensely at his hand. Heat bloomed where his palm pressed against Matthew's chest, seeping into his blood, and spreading throughout his body. That feeling of serenity returned, although neither of Finn's hands was glowing anymore. Matthew tightened his grip over the healer's hand, making sure it stayed in place.

"You are," Finn eventually admitted.

Matthew released a breath. "Why do you care so much?"

Finn met Matthew's gaze. His eyes glued the shifter to the spot, frozen by the clear, deep blue they possessed. There was so much emotion behind those eyes, flickering across the beautiful iris' like the pages of a book. Concern; fear; and anger, all mixed into a medley of open feelings, laid out bare for anyone to look at.

"I have seen too much death in my life...in that wretched circus. I couldn't bear the thought of someone else dying... Not when I could help." Finn's breath shook as he breathed in. "Not when that person was so kind to me."

Matthew listened carefully to Finn, his free hand subconsciously lifting and settling on top of the one holding onto Finn's. His heart was slamming against his ribcage, but he didn't care if the healer felt it. He hoped he did. There was nothing that made a person feel more alive than their body humming with the excitement of falling for someone.

"Each whipping scar," Finn's eyes fell to the hand that was encased in both of Matthew's, "represents a life I could not save. A reminder from the ringmaster to do… better next time."

Matthew remembered the marks he had seen on Finn's arms; the one that sat on the top of his hand; the many he had not seen. They were not just random acts of violence. They were given as reminders, and so served to Finn as symbols of lost lives. No wonder the thought of someone else dying repelled him. He was carrying around so many dead souls already, he did not need any more.

"I'm not dead," Matthew said firmly. "You saved me, remember?"

Finn made a dismissive noise. "I did nothing. Thursday saved you. Sybil, too. Whitney also saved you. If it were not for them, I would never have known. All I did was pop up at the end and heal some wounds. You weren't in any real danger once Charles released you. You were simply… damaged."

Matthew had to admit that there was truth to that. That didn't take away from what Finn had done for him, though.

"And you fixed me," Matthew answered.

Finn pulled a face. He couldn't resist chuckling. "That was such a bad line," he said.

Matthew grinned. "I'm full of bad lines," he said. "You haven't even heard the worst of my bad lines, yet."

"Are you sure? That angel one was pretty bad." Finn's smile fed Matthew's desire, causing the shifter to smile back until his cheeks hurt. "Do you use that on all the pretty...women?"

The confusion in Finn's tone amused Matthew. "I don't associate my flirtations through something as trivial as gender. Personality; actions; ambitions; everything that makes up a human, that's what's important. Everything else can come later. It's the soul that matters."

Finn's gaze shifted nervously away from Matthew's. "Have you made any kind of judgment on my soul, yet?"

It was such a big question. There was so much Matthew could tell Finn. How he admired him in every way, from his wild bronze hair to his wide cobalt eyes; from the way his face burned red whenever he was embarrassed to the laughter lines that appeared in his skin when he smiled. How he respected everything he stood for, from his ambition to heal and mend and cure the world, no matter who they were, to his determination to become a man of medicine despite his ability. How he respected him more than he had respected anyone in his life, because of how he turned his negative experiences into something positive and amazing.

Matthew could not say it, but Finn's soul was the most beautiful soul he had ever encountered. He cared for every inch, right down to the scars on his skin and the violet water on his neck.

"I want to know more of your soul," Matthew answered, his voice hushed as if people were listening in on them.

"There's not much to show," Finn replied.

Matthew smiled softly. "I doubt that."

Without any more preamble, before Finn could believe he was saying these things out of pity, Matthew pulled the healer into a close embrace.

Many people had come and gone throughout Matthew's life. He had kissed seasoned prostitutes; touched high society ladies; and slept with Dukes, Princes, and Counts. He had done so much, with so many colourful characters, all as a means of burying himself and hiding away from the truth he did not want to admit to himself. The truth was that he had always been nothing more than a product of what other people wanted. Those prostitutes; high society ladies; Dukes and Princes and Counts; none of them would have given him a second glance if they had seen him as he truly was, not how they wished him to be. Yet, he still found a high with them. Some level of pleasure he could take home with him each time.

None of that, none of it, amounted to anything compared to the feeling of holding Friday's Child in his arms.

No one saw him the way Finn did.

Matthew wasn't good at finding ways of describing things, and the first thing that came to mind was socks.

It was like when you can't find your other sock. You resign yourself to the fact that you might never find it again, and you will just have to match the remaining one with others, despite them being an odd pair. They don't fit together. It doesn't feel complete, but you can still wear them that way. They serve the purpose you need them for.

Then, one day, when you're looking under your bed, you find that other sock. You feel better; happier; more comfortable now that the pair fit together. You feel complete.

Finn's arms were warm like a fire blazing on a winter's morning. Matthew stayed still, his eyes peacefully closed, his hand still holding the healer's neck. He found more contentment with his arms around Finn than he had done with any woman or man he had ever been with. It was so sweet, so simple, that Matthew didn't wish to move.

Finn didn't pull away from him. He didn't rip himself away or slap Matthew for his forwardness. The pair of them simply sat there on Finn's bed, their bodies pressed together in a chaste embrace. To an outsider, it would have looked rather awkward; only passionate couples locked together in a public display of affection would have sat together in such a way for so long. Yet, Matthew had never felt more peaceful.

Their hands found each other, despite both of their eyes being closed, and their fingers interlocked. Like they had both had the same thought, at the same time and didn't need to word it because they knew that the other was thinking the same thing.

Matthew didn't know how long he could have sat this way, clinging to Finn's healing hands like a man clinging to the edge of a cliff by his fingertips. Even if they went undisturbed for hours; days; or weeks; pulling away would always be too soon.

Sudden impatient knocking at Finn's door ripped them apart. It was Finn who jumped, breaking their embrace, just as Sawyer entered the room.

Anger filled Matthew as he turned his head to glare at the intruder. He could tell from one look at Sawyer's face that he knew exactly what they had been doing before he entered. "Haven't you heard of waiting for permission to enter?" Matthew snapped.

"I was sent here to see if you were feeling any better," Sawyer said in his usual superior tone. He arched an eyebrow. "Looks like you're feeling *a lot* better."

Finn tensed. When Matthew looked at him, he saw him staring at the floor, an embarrassed crease between his eyebrows. The sight itself ignited a fire of a different kind inside his belly. "Stop talking down to us like that," Matthew snapped, returning his gaze to Sawyer.

Sawyer flicked his hair from his eyes, an amused smirk on his face. "I'm not talking down to Finn, I'm talking down to you, Matthew."

"Then don't talk down to him," Finn said. "You don't have any right to."

Matthew's mouth opened, but no words came out. Even Sawyer looked taken aback. He only let the surprise show on his face for a moment before he fixed it back into his usual mask of apathy.

"Look, there are people worried about you downstairs, will you come down already and let them know you're fine? If you have time to make a fool of yourself up here then you have plenty of time to come down and show the others that you were exaggerating last night," he said.

Matthew ground his teeth together, moving to stand up and retaliate, but was tugged back. He hadn't realised that Finn may have broken their hug, but he hadn't released one of his hands. He was now using the grip to hold him back.

Amused by Matthew's lack of fight, Sawyer left without saying anything else. He thought he had won the argument.

Matthew turned desperately to Finn, ready to complain about being held back, but the healer beat him to speaking.

"That is a man who craves a reaction. He pushes the buttons that he knows will get you angry. He wants you to yell at him. Don't give him the satisfaction of that," Finn said.

"How do you read people so easily?" Matthew asked incredulously.

Finn shrugged. "I guess it's just in my nature," he grinned.

Matthew's mouth curved into a smile. Finn was blushing one minute, defiant the next, then cheeky the next. Matthew didn't know what to expect and it kept him on his toes. It was one of the many reasons he found this man's company so enjoyable. There was never a dull moment.

"We should go downstairs," Matthew said. "I don't want to leave them worrying about me."

Finn nodded and climbed off the bed, Matthew following so they didn't have to let go of one another's hands just yet. He suddenly stopped, tugging Finn to a halt as well.

"I must apologise for my actions before the intrusion," Matthew said when Finn looked at him quizzically. Matthew's smile turned playful. "I didn't mean to be so forward. I couldn't help myself. If you'll allow, I would like to present my interest in a more civilised fashion."

Finn's eyebrows lifted, his cheeks staining pink at the mere mention of their hug. He cocked his head with interest and asked, "Oh? In what way?"

Matthew lifted their joined hands and placed a gentle kiss on top of Finn's. Their eyes never broke away from one another. Finn breathed out shakily as Matthew straightened and rubbed his thumb over the spot where his lips had just rested. "I know you're new to this world, and I don't wish to rush you. These things take time. This is me formally expressing my interest."

Finn stared at Matthew. "Your interest?" he repeated, completely baffled.

"To court. There's no pressure attached to this statement," Matthew assured. "Do with the information what you will."

"I… I don't know if I'm ready."

If Finn had been blushing before, then his entire face had caught fire now.

Matthew smirked devilishly. "That's okay. I'm a patient man. I can wait."

Finn's eyes were wide. Not with shock or horror, but more with disbelief. He slowly nodded, clearly unable to find the words to express his incredulity. The fact that he was so surprised that anyone could be interested in him warmed Matthew's heart. Matthew would never voice it out of fear of scaring Finn off, but at this very moment, he felt like he could wait until the end of the world.

"We should go," Matthew said. "Come, *mon Cherie.*"

As he turned, Finn said from behind him, "You know French. Sure. Okay. *Naturally.*"

Matthew laughed. He was so elated, that he practically skipped out of Finn's room.

It didn't last.

When he entered the sitting room, the air was thick with concern. Everyone was there, except for Sawyer. Even Ophelia had joined them, breaking her habit of hiding in her bedroom. They resembled a family waiting on a doctor's verdict in a hospital. In a twisted way, Matthew supposed that both scenarios did ring true to one another. Finn was practically a doctor, and these people were their family.

Thursday was the first to react. "You didn't die!" she exclaimed, jumping to her feet. "I said so, didn't I? Of course, he wasn't going to die!"

"I did say that death was highly unlikely," Finn reminded her.

"People have died over less," Whitney stated.

Matthew caught Whitney's eye, but she quickly looked away. Like Finn, she had dark bags under her eyes. Had she not slept either? Finn had said that she had been extremely worried about him, but surely not so much so that she hadn't been able to sleep. It was jarring to consider. Whitney had always been so reserved; so closed off; so secluded; the thought of her not being able to sleep because she was worried about him was strange. Especially since it was *him*. The most annoying person under Sybil's roof.

"I'm so glad you're okay," Sybil said, getting up from her seat and wrapping her arms around Matthew's neck.

"Thanks, Sybil," Matthew replied, smiling into her shoulder.

"I'm so sorry about Charles, Matthew," Ophelia said desperately, also standing. "I didn't think he'd know... I didn't think he'd attempt to kill other people just to get to me."

Matthew met Ophelia's gaze over Sybil's shoulder. He couldn't tell if she had seen him shift last night or not. Judging by how she didn't look afraid of him, and it wasn't the first thing she had brought up, she couldn't have. Surely, she had seen Sybil dragging Charles away and witnessed Thursday flying and blowing chunks out of the wall. Maybe she had chalked what she remembered down to shock or decided that she had dreamed of the supernatural elements.

"I'm glad he found me before you," Matthew answered.

"We need to talk about what to do with Charles," Sybil explained as she released Matthew.

Thursday's hand immediately shot into the air.

"*Without* killing him," Sybil said pointedly.

Thursday's hand fell again.

"There's no point reporting him to the police," Ophelia said despondently. "Those two men helping him last night were friends of his from the force. How do we know who is in allegiance with him and who isn't? Thursday was followed back here simply because she inquired about him. How that made them jump to the conclusion that I was here, I don't know, but it happened."

Matthew leaned against the door. He had figured that the two men he had killed were friends from the force. Ophelia was right. There was no way to know who at the station were genuine officers and who were friends of Charles.'

"I think we should just let him rot in our basement. His friends are already dead," Thursday said, folding her arms with finality. "If he's trapped down there, Ophelia can live her life free of him."

"That is practically murder. His friends were killed in self-defence," Sybil exclaimed. "You'd have his blood on your hands."

Thursday shrugged. "I can live with that."

"Where is the justice in that?" Titus asked.

"Justice is Ophelia getting to live her life without getting strangled like Matthew!" Thursday threw back. "And we all know that if it had been Ophelia, he would have thrown her over the bannister!"

Finn had been shaking his head the entire time Thursday had been speaking. "You're willing to reduce yourself to the same level as a homicidal abuser and dare to call it justice?"

Thursday's eyebrows lifted then furrowed. "Sometimes you gotta step on some toes to achieve what you want," she answered.

"This isn't stepping on toes. You're talking about murder!"

Thursday glowered. "Look, *healer*, you're new here, so let me let you in on a secret: don't argue with me, you'll lose," she said. "This isn't a church meeting; you're going to have to get off your podium of morals if you're going to cope with us."

"Don't let her intimidate you, Finn, she thinks she's scarier than she is," Titus assured.

This made Thursday look to Titus. She bared her teeth in a wide grin, "I can be scary," she said through her clenched teeth. Matthew thought she looked terrifying baring her mouth in such a way, like a feral animal threatening to bite. Titus, however, did not look one bit impressed. The man had seen a helluva lot more in his life than Matthew had done, so his unhinged sister exposing her teeth at him was nothing but a drop in the ocean.

"If you're asking me to abandon my principles to 'cope' then I'm sorry to tell you that I am not interested," Finn explained, also not at all concerned by Thursday's dental display. "There were times when my principles were all I had. If I didn't abandon them then, I most certainly am not abandoning them now."

Thursday eyed Finn through narrowed eyes. "What principles?"

"Pacifism."

That word alone was enough to make Thursday groan. She threw herself into her chair dramatically, slinging her arm over her eyes. "You're going to complain about everything I want to do!" she complained.

Sybil was grinning. "You continue to be outnumbered," she informed Thursday.

"Sawyer would agree with me!"

"Sawyer isn't here," Matthew dutifully pointed out.

He enjoyed hearing Finn participate in their group's discussions. One reason being that it saved Matthew himself from talking too much. Titus only ever interjected occasionally, and Whitney could be as quiet as the dead when she wanted, so sometimes there would be silences that followed Thursday or Sybil, the most outspoken in the group besides Sawyer (but the nature of his opinions caused Matthew to think that he didn't count). Matthew usually felt obligated to fill these silences. Now Finn was arguing with genuine points. With Thursday, of all people.

Matthew was almost afraid of how much he liked this man.

Thursday sighed heavily. "What do you propose we do with Charles then, *healer*?"

"OCPD," Finn answered.

Everyone stared at the healer. Even Matthew had no idea what Finn was talking about. "What?" he asked.

Finn waved his hands around in a vague gesture towards the door. "Opara City Police Department. Can anyone drive? If someone can get to Opara City, then they can report Charles to them. Explain what is going on with Castlebrooke's Police Department. I don't see why they wouldn't send someone down to investigate."

A pause.

"That... could work," Titus said. He sounded surprised. Matthew assumed that Titus couldn't believe that he hadn't thought of such a logical answer himself.

Thursday perked up. "Can I drive there?"

"*No*, Thursday," Sybil said. "I will." As Thursday slouched in disappointment, their leader looked to Finn, "Good thinking, Finn."

The idea of Thursday behind the wheel of a car was terrifying, but for Sybil it made sense. In classic Sybil fashion, when cars became available to those with deep enough pockets, she had to teach herself how they worked. She bought her own vehicle-using Sawyer as a front so no questions were asked about what a woman would want with a car-and spent weeks reading papers and books about their function and production. Matthew didn't know where she found the energy for so much work. He didn't know how she had any room left in her brain. Thursday must have had similar thoughts, as she didn't teach herself how to drive. She just assumed that she would figure it out along the way.

"I can go if you wish," Finn volunteered. Matthew looked at the man with surprise. Could *he* drive?

"No, no, you're still hurt," Sybil replied, gesturing to the cane still in Finn's hand. "If I go now, I can be in Opara City by morning." She was already gathering her hair up into a bun so that she could stuff it into a hat. Sybil drove around on main roads more than she should for someone without an official licence. As ridiculous as it sounded, she was less likely to be stopped if she passed as a man.

"Be careful, Sybil," Matthew said.

Sybil grinned, a lock of ginger hair falling into her eye as she tied the rest into place. "Thank you. I'll try to get there as fast as I can, but I'll be safe, of course. No point in being reckless. Charles isn't going anywhere anyways."

Ophelia approached Sybil and embraced her. "I can't tell you how much this means to me," she whispered. "I can't thank you enough."

"It's the least we can do," Sybil answered, patting Ophelia's back. She pulled back with a smile and winked. "I'll see you guys soon."

Matthew followed Sybil out of the sitting room. She went to the hat rack and stuffed her hair into a dull brown cap. "Sybil," he began, "this means so much to me... It should be me going to Opara City, not you..."

Sybil laughed and turned to face him. Her hair was not the sort that liked being tamed. Strands of orange were peeking out of the brim of the cap but, from a distance, she would pass as a male. "You would be in more danger out there than I ever would be," she said. "Imagine a policeman stopping you in the Meadows in the middle of the night. Those stories of disappearances might become true, and I don't intend to lose you just yet, Mister."

Matthew's lips twitched. He didn't know how to react to such care. He had never known his mother so until Thursday had brought him here, he had never had a parental figure in his life. Sybil, besides Finn, was the only person to let Matthew know how much she cared about him. She cared about all the people she had taken in. He was thankful for having her in his life.

"I should still be going," Matthew told her.

Sybil smiled softly. "Look, Matthew, regardless of how this started, I think that sooner or later Charles would have attempted to kill Ophelia. Their relationship, or what she has told me of it, was not at all healthy. It would have only been a matter of time. Now she might have a chance at living. And that's because of you. Or, Samuel, if you like."

Matthew tried to be comforted by this, but he still felt like there was something he could be doing. If only he were able to leave this damn house. He was enslaved to his ability.

Seeing the frustration on the shifter's face, Sybil put her hand on his shoulder. "How about when I get back and the OCPD has taken care of Charles, we focus more intensely on conquering your shifts?"

Matthew nodded. "I'd like that," he said.

Sybil patted his cheek. "Good man," she said. "Now I've got to go if I have any hope of reaching the city by tomorrow. Will you be okay?"

"Oh, don't worry about me, I'll be fine," Matthew told her, forcing a smile.

With one final reassuring smile, Sybil turned and moved to the door. She grabbed one of Sawyer's coats off the rack and threw it on as she left.

Matthew stood in the silence that followed. He wished that he could be as selfless as Sybil. She gave what she had for others without thinking twice about it, seeing the best in everyone until they proved themselves to be irretrievable. Anyone who could hold down a relationship with a sordid man such as Sawyer must have an amazing amount of patience. Matthew only wished he could share his time and energy without thought, knowing that he wouldn't be getting anything in return.

In many ways, Matthew looked up to Sybil. He aspired to be like her someday. He *hoped* he could be like her someday.

"Hey, Matthew?"

Titus had come out of the living room. Matthew raised his eyebrows, "Yeah?" he asked. Besides lecturing, Titus didn't start up conversation with him often.

Titus didn't look Matthew in the eye, instead directing his eyes to the floor. He tugged on his earlobe nervously and said,

"I, uh, I just wanted to let you know that I prayed for you last night. To recover, I mean."

Here he was again, left speechless.

Matthew had never been a man of God. He had never been a man of any faith. He didn't mind others practising what they wanted, though, especially if it gave them comfort or happiness. If they didn't try to force it onto him or lecture him about God's word or whatever it was that they preached about, then Matthew didn't care. Titus tended to preach a lot, hence why Matthew's first instinct when hearing the word 'religion' was to roll his eyes.

Despite this, Matthew knew what it meant to pray for people. For Titus, praying was a big deal. Titus believed that praying worked if enough passion and energy were put into it. This meant that upon hearing the news that Matthew had been hurt last night, Titus had gathered all his passion; his energy; and his faith to pray to his God for Matthew to recover.

"Thank you," Matthew managed to say. His voice was quiet as he was still attempting to comprehend what Titus had just told him.

"I'm glad Finn was able to heal you," Titus said.

He stuck his hand out and Matthew realised he wanted him to shake it. Matthew did without hesitation.

As he watched Titus ascend the stairs, Matthew found himself questioning how much he knew about the people he was living with. The two people he thought didn't care about him in the slightest had both been distressed by what Charles had done to him and acted against it in the only way they knew how. Titus hadn't even tried to tell Matthew that his recovery was all because of God and his prayers because he knew Matthew didn't like being lectured in that way.

How could he live with these people for so long and barely know anything about them?

The living room doors flew open again. When Finn came out, Matthew's heart skipped a beat. It was only momentary as it became apparent that the healer was being followed out.

"Look, all I'm asking is that you give the 'never raise your hand' rubbish a rest now and then," Thursday was insisting, hot on Finn's heels. "I know there's some hullabaloo about when someone hits you offer the other cheek or something, but you've got to believe me when I say it doesn't always work!"

Finn caught Matthew's eye as he passed, and they exchanged a smile.

"You're thinking about the bible, Thursday. Pacifism isn't a religion, it's simply a way of living," Finn explained. He didn't look around, knowing that Thursday was following him to the stairs. "And it has worked pretty well for me so far."

Matthew rotated on his heel to watch Finn's journey to the stairs, Thursday in close pursuit.

"I don't believe that," Thursday was saying. "Anyone with a brain knows that violence fixes everything. Quite quickly, too."

"Maybe I don't have a brain then," was Finn's response. "Now, I'm heading to the bathroom, unless you care to join me there, I'd say your journey ends here."

Thursday snorted. "You have much to learn, healer."

Matthew snickered as Thursday rounded on Finn and slung her arm around his neck, making it clear that she had no problem following him to the lavatory. As they went up the stairs, her arm slid down to the middle of his back to aid him up the stairs in the same way that Matthew had done. It was sweet to watch Thursday helping Finn. Even if it was just so that she could continue pestering him about his beliefs.

Matthew shook his head with amusement and turned to enter the living room again.

Ophelia's head popped out, halting him.

"Hey," she said, sliding out into the foyer. "Is there anywhere that we can talk?"

Matthew was surprised by this request, but he tried not to show it on his face. "Yes, of course."

Matthew led Ophelia to one of the empty living rooms. Many went unused, mainly because Sybil's house was built to house more than seven people. If it had been a better day, he would have taken her out into the garden. He didn't like the empty rooms. They were so cold and bare. It felt wrong.

This room sat on the edge of the house, overlooking the vast garden that lay beyond. It wasn't empty, there was furniture scattered in basic formation, all covered with white sheets. It put Matthew in mind of a room someone had been murdered in. No one dared enter, so everything inside was covered up to be preserved.

When they entered, Matthew went straight to the window. The rain was beating the glass, sliding down the pane like spilt paint. He sat down on the window bench. Ophelia didn't need to be told to follow. She wordlessly seated herself beside him.

There was a pregnant silence as the pair sat and pondered their next move. Matthew was worried about what Ophelia wanted to talk to him about. He didn't know why. There was nothing she could surely say to him that would be cause for worry.

"I saw you last night," Ophelia eventually said.

Matthew looked at her quizzically. "Excuse me?"

Ophelia inhaled. The dull light from outside made her pale skin stand out like it had been polished. "I saw you… change last night."

A lump formed in Matthew's throat. "Oh?" he croaked.

"I saw that purple light come from Thursday's hands. Sybil dragged my husband across the floor without touching him,"

Ophelia continued. She threw a sharp look at Matthew. "Don't dare tell me that I'm mad. I know what I saw. Charles didn't try to murder you for no reason, did he?"

"Ar-are y-you sure y-you weren't just tired?" Matthew stammered. "Our minds can be powerful things and they run wild when we're sleep deprived"-

"What did I say?" Ophelia snapped. "I know what I saw."

Matthew sighed in defeat. He didn't see the use in lying to her. He could try to convince her that she was going insane, but what would that achieve? Besides, Ophelia wasn't the sort of woman who would allow herself to be spoken down to by a man like him. She knew what she saw. When faced with something so surreal in reality, you know that you can't make it up.

"No. Charles didn't just attack me for no reason."

Ophelia's breath shook. She nodded. "Tell me then. What are you? What are all of you?"

He had never been faced with this question before. Matthew searched helplessly for an answer in his head. "We're just people," he pathetically replied. "We're just people who got cursed with abilities we didn't ask for. Ultimately, we are as human as you or as Charles."

Ophelia shook her head. "You're better people than Charles."

Matthew fixed her with a confused look. "You aren't frightened?"

"Do I have reason to be?" Ophelia enquired. She placed her hand against the window, the glass around her fingers immediately beginning to fog up. "All you have done since I arrived at your home is try to protect me. Abilities or not, you've kept me safe. If you intended to hurt me, why is Sybil currently on her way to Opara City to have my husband arrested, risking her safety in the process? Why would you risk your own life to ensure that Charles didn't find me last night if you wanted me dead? You would have killed me the first night I arrived if you had truly intended to hurt me."

Matthew couldn't dispute her logic. The only contradicting reasoning he could come up with was that they could have been fattening her up like that witch in that fairy tale. That, however, was too ridiculous, even for him to suggest.

"Why did Charles try to kill you?" Ophelia asked.

"When, ah, someone first looks at me, they see who they desire the most," Matthew sheepishly explained. It felt strange, to explain his ability to a human. Moreover, a human he had used his ability on. "When Charles looked at me, he saw... you..."

Ophelia was silent for a moment, absorbing what she had been told. She eventually frowned. "I did not see who I desired most," she said.

"Ah, well, sometimes it doesn't work," Matthew lied.

"Why do I not believe you?"

"I don't know. That's your choice."

Ophelia's eyes were narrowed with disbelief, but she didn't push the matter any further. "Is Samuel gifted also?"

How was he supposed to answer that? Matthew couldn't make anything up that would sound believable, but he also couldn't let her know that he was Samuel. She would be disturbed, surely.

Matthew feigned ignorance. "Pardon?"

"Is Samuel also gifted?" Ophelia patiently repeated.

Matthew averted his gaze and focused on the garden beyond the window. The grass was a bright contrast against the boring grey sky. If he squinted, he could make out the many assorted colours of Whitney's flower beds in the distance. He wondered if she had planted any violets recently. He had grown to like the smell.

"Matthew?" Ophelia pressed. Her voice was stern. She clearly didn't like her questions going unanswered.

Matthew wanted to answer her, but he didn't know how to. He couldn't find the right words to explain away Samuel's existence.

"I have a feeling," Ophelia quietly said, "that there is something that you are not telling me."

He couldn't look her in the eye. He continued to stare out the window and began to chew on his bottom lip anxiously.

Beside him, there was an intake of breath.

"Samuel chewed his lip like that," Ophelia murmured. "He also had the snarky attitude that you have."

Matthew cringed, his reflection mockingly cringing back at him.

Ophelia touched his shoulder. "Matthew? Please tell me that I'm not insane. Please tell me that he's still here, in a way. I already feel so crazy, please inject even a little bit of sanity back into my life."

Matthew huffed out a tired breath and glanced at Ophelia. As soon as their eyes met, his gaze gave him away, just like he knew that it would. Ophelia's hands flew to her mouth, and she gasped. Matthew waited for it. He waited for her to start yelling obscenities; to be disgusted; to even hit out at him. He understood. It would be a natural response.

Instead, his body was thrust against the window and there were lips on top of his own.

Matthew didn't know how to respond. It was like his brain had malfunctioned and he simply sat there in shock. Ophelia was kissing him. Why was she kissing him? Why wasn't she shocked, disturbed, or disgusted? Was this her way of expressing her disgust? No, that didn't make any sense whatsoever.

Ophelia's face fell into his chest, and she hugged him. "I'm so happy that you're safe!" she cried. "I thought that Charles had surely killed you!"

"Uh…" Words wouldn't reach Matthew's dumbfounded mouth. He didn't know what to say or do, or even think. This was not the type of reaction he had been expecting.

Ophelia pulled away from their embrace and started fixing his hair like a fussing mother. "I knew that there was a reason that you were acting so strange when I first arrived. Thursday played it off better than you did. No wonder. You probably don't get faced with this brand of trouble every day."

Matthew was still shocked, his lips damp from where Ophelia had thrown her own at them. "Aren't you disgusted?" he managed to ask.

Ophelia was taken aback by such a suggestion. "Why in the world would I be disgusted?"

Matthew stood up. "Surely, you know why," he insisted. "It's dishonest. Deceptive, even. You were upfront with me about everything, even about your husband. I wasn't"-

"What could you have done?" Ophelia asked. "Told me that you were magical? Or had special abilities? Do you honestly believe that would have worked if I had not witnessed it with my own eyes?"

Matthew pulled a face. "I could have at least told you that my name wasn't Samuel."

"Matthew, you are the only person berating yourself here," Ophelia answered. She stood up and took his hands into her own. "You are a good person. You don't have control of your... gift... yet. I cannot blame you for something that you have no control over. Neither should you."

"I'm trying to get it under control," Matthew felt the need to tell her. "Sybil has been helping me. It just hasn't... worked out yet."

Ophelia nodded in understanding. "I'm glad," she said. She didn't release his hands. She seemed to be studying his face like she was trying to commit it to memory. Matthew was used to people looking at him intensely-it was in the job description of his ability-but it was different when it was his natural face that was being scrutinized.

"Uh," he stupidly said, "you okay?"

Ophelia did not beat around the bush. "Does this mean that once Charles is in prison, we could continue our relationship?"

The question threw Matthew off guard. He stared at her with wide eyes, silent as the dead. Words didn't seem to reach his mouth. Ophelia did not look at all embarrassed by her question. She quirked an eyebrow at him, awaiting his response.

Matthew liked Ophelia, he really did, but there was a reason that he didn't have long-term relationships with humans. He couldn't court them properly, not when he didn't have control of his ability yet. Not only would it put him in danger, but it would put them in danger, too. It was too risky. He had accepted his fate as a lonely bachelor long ago.

"I don't think so," Matthew stammered. "I'm sorry," he added for good measure.

Ophelia narrowed her eyes. "Why not?"

"Trust me, it's better for the both of us. I'm flattered that you would wish to continue what we had, but you have got to believe me when I say that it would not work out," Matthew quickly explained.

"So, you just have one-night stands?" Ophelia's voice wasn't judgemental, it was just flat. She released his hands and stepped away from him.

Matthew shrugged wearily. "It's all I can do."

Ophelia didn't look too amused by his response. It was possible that she wasn't accustomed to being rejected in such a manner. "I see," was all she said.

"I'm sorry," Matthew said again.

Ophelia held a hand up to stop him from going on. She firmly changed the subject, unable to bear to listen to Matthew justify his rejection. "I'm assuming that Thursday; Sybil and you aren't the only ones gifted. Who else is?"

"All of us," Matthew answered, carefully eyeing Ophelia like she was about to explode any moment. He cast his gaze to the door, hoping that Thursday hadn't decided to come looking for him and was eavesdropping. It would not be the first time that he opened a door and had her topple into the room.

Ophelia's face was alight with curiosity. "What can the others do?"

"Uh, Titus is agile. He never falls. Kind of like a cat? It's difficult to explain. He's graceful, kind of bendy too." Matthew scratched his head. "Finn can heal. Sawyer can manipulate fate"-

"Fate is in the hands of that man?" Ophelia looked extremely disturbed. Matthew didn't blame her. He was disturbed by Sawyer's ability every day of the week.

"Not complete fate. He can just sort of play around with certain elements to make things go as he wishes them to go. It doesn't work all the time and from what I gather it takes an awful lot of concentration for it to work," Matthew explained.

Ophelia didn't look comforted by this. She didn't question any further, probably wanting to move the conversation away from Sawyer as quickly as possible. "And what about Whitney? There's a reason why she's always in her room, isn't there?"

Matthew nodded. "At the moment, she is extremely dangerous. It's not her fault. She can manipulate the elements, but what element she can manipulate depends on the mood that she is in. If she ever got too angry, she could burn this entire house down. That's why she spends most of her time alone. She's working on it, though. Sybil is helping her."

For the first time since the conversation started, Ophelia looked scared. Matthew didn't like that this was the reaction Whitney usually evoked in people. Despite her surly demeanour, she wasn't someone to be feared. She would never intentionally harm an innocent person.

Thinking on his feet, Matthew turned Ophelia around to face the window. "Do you see that colourful patch in the garden there? Near the gates?"

Ophelia leaned forward and squinted. "Yes," she answered.

"That's Whitney's flower beds. When she feels neutral, she controls the earth. She uses that time to grow flowers in the garden," Matthew explained. "If she had the choice, I think she would spend all of her time out there."

Ophelia was silent for a moment. "Are you not afraid that I'll go and tell the world about what you are?"

"I don't mean this in a rude way, but who would believe you? Besides Charles, of course," Matthew answered.

They wouldn't even have had to worry about Charles going and telling the world about them. All such ravings would earn a person was a one-way ticket to United Arms Asylum. Matthew could tell that Ophelia knew this, too. She had just asked the question to see how he would answer her.

"You have nothing to fear. No one here will hurt you," Matthew assured her.

Ophelia nodded slowly. "Yes, I believe you," she replied.

She wearily cast another glance out the window before sighing. It was a heavy sound, like the burden of the information she had been given weighed down her vocal cords.

"If you don't mind, I'm going to go to bed. After last night, I feel exhausted," she said.

"Oh yes, of course," Matthew replied. "Go ahead."

He wasn't feeling extremely tired himself, but that could have been down to Finn's healing. Finn had yet to fully explain the parameters and limits of his ability. For all Matthew knew, he wouldn't sleep for a month because being healed gave him some sort of energy overload.

Matthew watched Ophelia leave the room. As soon as the door shut behind her, he deflated. The conversation had gone a lot better than he thought it would. He had expected Ophelia to be disgusted, or disturbed at the very least, yet she was neither of those things.

She had been willing to continue their . . . whatever it was that they had. Matthew couldn't tell whether she was insane or did not care about what he looked like. Surely, she did. She had fallen for Samuel, not Matthew. Yet, she had still asked. Maybe it was just the stress from the previous night making her want human closeness. Being confronted by someone who wants to kill you can be extremely daunting and can make a person act irrationally.

She didn't seem overly annoyed by being turned down. Sure, she had looked a little bothered when he initially explained why to her, but once they got into the conversation about the others' abilities, she seemed to forget all about it. Matthew hoped it didn't prey on her mind too much. It was nothing personal to her, it was simply better for them both that they didn't have a relationship. It would be too complicated, and Ophelia didn't deserve that. After everything she had endured, she deserved an easy future.

Besides, as awful as it sounded, Matthew didn't know if he wanted to court Ophelia even if his ability hadn't been in the way. There was a time when he would have jumped on the opportunity. Maybe blaming his ability was just an excuse.

An attempt to save Ophelia's feelings because he had not wanted to tell her that he was interested in someone else.

CHAPTER TEN

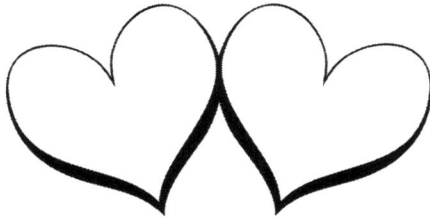

MATTHEW COULDN'T FOCUS ON ANYTHING WHILE KNOWING THAT SYBIL WAS TRAVELLING TO OPARA CITY. This manifested itself in sitting on the foyer stairs, simply staring at the doors. He had somehow convinced himself that if he stared at them, it would hasten her safe return. He knew that Sybil could handle herself, but that didn't lessen his worry any. What if she couldn't convince the police? What if she got into trouble for driving? What if she got lost in the dark? There were so many possibilities for things to go wrong that it made Matthew feel nauseous.

"Look out!"

Matthew looked over his shoulder just in time to catch Thursday flying down the bannister like a child. She leapt off at the end in a flurry of dark hair and blue dress skirts. She stalked over to him, a pleased smirk on her face. "What in the world are you doing?" she asked.

"Waiting," Matthew answered.

"Uh-huh," Thursday sceptically replied. "What for?"

"Sybil."

Thursday threw herself onto the step below Matthew. "You know she's going to be fine, right?"

"Yes. I just can't focus on anything else."

Thursday hummed. Not in agreement but understanding. "The sooner that man is out of this house, the better. The sooner Ophelia can get on, the better. She's alright but I can't say I'm fond of her."

"Why not?" Matthew frowned.

"I don't know. Some people I just don't like," Thursday shrugged. "She gives me a bad feeling."

Matthew supposed that was fair enough, but he was curious as to why Thursday didn't like Ophelia. Then again, Thursday didn't need a lot of reason not to like someone. Matthew remembered her once declaring that she despised the local butcher because he had cut the meat that she had ordered wrong.

"You need a distraction," Thursday concluded.

"It won't work," Matthew stated before she had even proposed what she had in mind.

Thursday glared at him. "Have you bedded Finn yet?" she asked.

This immediately snatched Matthew's attention. His head snapped to look down at the woman below him. "What?" he nervously laughed. "No!"

Thursday had asked this question to get a reaction, and she had gotten exactly what she wanted. She rolled her eyes and groaned. "I knew it," she complained.

"Knew what?" Matthew demanded.

"You've caught the feelings." Thursday reached up and slapped his cheek like an appraising aunt. "I thought you were better than that, Matthew."

"I haven't caught anything!" Matthew deflected. "I've no idea what you're talking about."

"Oh please, I'm not an idiot. You look at the healer with more admiration than Sybil would even spare Sawyer," said Thursday. "You don't want to bed him because doing something so flippant doesn't merit the emotions you have grown to feel towards him. You don't want to ruin what is most likely his first time with a man like yourself by tricking him into your bed. You're pretty easy to read sometimes, Matthew."

Matthew's heart pounded in his chest. Was he so transparent?

"What if I told you that you were wrong?"

Thursday turned and knelt on the stair she had previously sat on so that they were looking one another in the eyes. "*Am I wrong?*"

Her eyes were very intimidating. There was something in those chocolate brown iris' that made Matthew uncomfortable. Especially when they were pointed at him in such a prying manner. Thursday had so many layers surrounding her, that it was difficult to decipher so much as a simple gaze.

When he didn't answer, Thursday clicked her tongue. "I knew it," she said.

Matthew shook his head. "Why is there never anything more to me beyond thinking about relationships?" he muttered.

"Well, up until this point, you technically only thought about sex," Thursday pointed out. "Because you always changed your face. Since you have always been forced to change who you are to suit the tastes of others, I think it's perfectly natural to be thinking about a relationship with Finn. Despite my disapproval."

"You disapprove of Finn?" Matthew frowned.

"No, I disapprove of relationships," Thursday corrected. "Emotions are dangerous. It is what defines us as beings of sentient thought, but it also detriments us. I was thrown into an asylum because my parents were terrified of how emotionless

I could be. Then again, it's not common to be able to switch them on and off like I can."

Matthew didn't want to know what Thursday was like when she switched her emotions off. She was already capable of being so ruthless; so threatening; so uncaring, that if Thursday decided to switch off her emotions one day, then she would be a complete danger to society. She was already a complete danger to society, so who could even imagine what an emotionless Thursday would do to the world?

"Relationships... they're like extra weight to carry. Suddenly, you're not just responsible for yourself, you're responsible for another person. Not out of obligation, but out of want," Thursday explained.

"Don't you consider your ties to the six of us relationships?" Matthew asked.

Thursday shrugged. "I mean, you don't exactly set my blood aflame," she answered. "No offence."

"None taken."

"What I'm trying to say is that it's different," Thursday insisted. "You guys were thrown into my life. What you're thinking of is *allowing* someone into your life. In a much more vulnerable way. Relationships aren't just a kiss and a cuddle, you know. They aren't about popping out kids, especially in this case, to keep a positive societal image. Courting someone means that you're going to be letting another person see your dirty laundry; your annoying habits; your insecurities. Are you prepared to do that?"

Matthew had not thought about it that way before. He didn't know how he had thought about it. He had never courted anyone before. Fleeting nights with people he never saw again was all he knew. A month ago, what Thursday had described would have sounded impossible for someone like him. After everything that had happened, including Ophelia's return and Finn's arrival, Matthew felt like he had a chance. This was an opportunity he might never get again. Matthew didn't *want* it to happen again, because that would imply that someone who wasn't Finn had come along, and Matthew didn't want anyone else. Finn was the first to see him as he was, no one else would ever compare to that.

"Yes," Matthew answered. "I am."

Thursday huffed, blowing her hair out of her eyes. "I thought you would say that." She raised an interested eyebrow. "You should take him to a molly house."

Matthew narrowed his eyes. "No," he said firmly.

Thursday snickered. "Aw, why not? I'm sure he'd love Adelia's place. He would fit right in!"

"No, he wouldn't, and you know why he wouldn't? He has never been in that type of environment before. Christ, he hadn't even openly admitted to being gay until my ability forced it from him," Matthew ranted.

"Look," Thursday said, thoroughly amused by how irritated she had made him, "he's not going to get any more used to the prospect being shut up in here now, is he?"

"You don't get it." Matthew stood up and leaned against the bannister, his jaw set. "Not everyone is as desensitised as you are, Thursday. Believe it or not, for a lot of people, liking the same sex in this day and age is an extremely daunting thing."

Thursday pulled a face. "Is that so? How quaint."

Matthew turned his head, looking to the front doors again. "You're right about one thing," he admitted.

"I'm right about everything, you're going to have to be a bit more specific," Thursday immediately answered.

"I'm not going to ruin his first experience-whether it is with me or someone else-by tricking him into bed or overwhelming him at Adelia Day's damned molly house." Matthew breathed heavily through his nose.

Thursday slung herself to her feet. She pretended to dust off her skirts as she stepped closer to Matthew. "Well, if you want my opinion, I think you're absolutely mad. More insane than I was when I was thrown into United Arms," she said.

Matthew rolled his eyes, preparing to retaliate with a snarky remark, when a heavy hand clamped down on his shoulder. Thursday's fingers dug into his skin as she squeezed him.

"I will admit, however, that you have had a certain… glow about you since Finn arrived," Thursday explained. "I'm happy that you are happy."

Matthew looked at Thursday quizzically. "I didn't think you cared for anyone's happiness except for your own."

His words made Thursday quirk an eyebrow. "Look, Matthew, since the day I found you crying in that apple tree, you've had this… heavy aura around you. Like you're constantly preparing for having to change again." Thursday rolled her head around on her neck. "And not for this to be construed like I actually care or anything but it's nice to see that lifted. It's like Finn distracts you from your ability. I think you've always needed that."

No matter how much Thursday tried to convince him otherwise, Matthew was construing this as caring. There were rumours around the mansion that Thursday had a heart beneath the thick skin she always wore. Very rarely, if you are in the right place at the right time, she lets you see it.

Thursday grinned. "Just remember that my room is still next door to yours. I hear everything, and I am always listening."

Matthew rolled his eyes. "Of course, how could I forget?"

The madwoman snickered and looped her arm through Matthew's. "Now come," she said. "Whitney is preparing dinner."

~M~

Thursday and Matthew were the last to enter the kitchen, working on the assumption that Sawyer wasn't going to bother; an assumption Matthew worked from regularly.

"So, what's for tea?" Thursday declared, hopping onto one of Whitney's worktops and sending carrots tumbling everywhere.

"Stew," Whitney answered shortly.

"Mmm, vegetable mush," Thursday mused sarcastically.

Whitney whipped her wooden spoon threateningly in Thursday's face, an unamused expression on her face. "Want to cook for yourself, then?"

Thursday clapped her hands together. "Me? Oh, I wouldn't dare try to compete with you!" She grinned and took a bite out of a raw carrot.

Titus studied Thursday from where he sat at the table. From what Matthew could see, it looked like he had been playing cards with Finn before they arrived. "Was that washed?" he asked with bemusement.

Thursday glanced at the carrot in her hand; shrugged; and took another bite.

Even Matthew had to turn his nose up. "That's disgusting," he groaned, snatching the dirty vegetable from his friend before she could steal another bite. "Didn't your mother ever tell you that eating unwashed vegetables will cause a vegetable to grow in your stomach?"

"No, my Mum was too busy scraping me off the bedroom walls every night," Thursday responded. Matthew supposed that made sense. He had not even been told such a thing by his mother; it was something he had heard the kids at the orphanage saying once. "She also prayed for my soul a lot. You would have liked her, Titus."

"Praying does not immediately equate decency of character," Titus disputed.

Matthew slapped his forehead. "So, *that's* why you're such a pain in the ass!" he smirked.

The look he got from Titus in response to this was hilarious, but Matthew could tell that Titus knew that he was kidding.

"Do you always do the cooking, Whitney?" Finn asked, trying to change the subject before the conversation spiralled into the controversial depths of religious debate.

"We used to have a daily rota," Whitney explained as she started plating up the stew. "But between Thursday nearly poisoning us; Matthew not knowing anything to do with cooking; and Sawyer's experimental dishes, it was eventually decided that I was the best person to do it."

"I knew some things," Matthew argued. He didn't want to look pathetically incompetent.

Whitney looked at him plainly. "You didn't even know how the potato peeler worked."

"Okay, apart from that"-

"You nearly cored your thumb with the apple corer."

"That was a minor setback"-

"You left a kitchen towel on top of the gas!"

"Alright, alright!" Matthew relented.

Someone snickered. Matthew turned in the direction of the sound. A smile infected his face when Finn ducked his head and covered his mouth, clearly trying to hide that he was the one who had laughed.

"Here, make yourselves useful," Whitney instructed, shoving a bowl into Thursday's hands and then into Matthew's. "Give out the food."

They ate in silence. Not because conversation was lacking, but because Whitney's stew was so good. Matthew didn't know where she had learned to cook but he wasn't going to complain about it. It certainly beat Thursday's questionably coloured meat and Sawyer's unrecognisable mass of lumpy liquid.

While he was helping Titus clear up, Matthew was accosted by Thursday at the sink.

"Hey!" she hissed, jumping in his way.

"What?" Matthew exclaimed, stopping himself from dropping a bowl in shock.

"Give me those," Thursday demanded. She snatched the bowls out of Matthew's arms before he could protest. "You have more important business to be attending to."

"Oh? And what's that?" Matthew was both confused and concerned by Thursday's uncharacteristic helpfulness. He was going to remain on guard until she proved that he didn't have to be.

"You're going to take Finn out," Thursday grinned.

Matthew rolled his eyes. "I've told you, Thursday, I won't put him into that situation"-

"Not Adelia Day's," Thursday whisper hissed. "Surely you have places where you take your partners to be alone."

"Plenty of places, but that's beside the point"-

"No, it's not," Thursday quickly interrupted. "Take him out. He's been cooped inside this mansion ever since he was brought here. It's the outdoors, not a sweat-infested molly house. He will thank you."

Matthew glanced over to the table. Finn was gathering up the cards he and Titus had been playing their game with. He kept having to brush his hair out of his eyes, the tanned locks refusing to cooperate.

"I've never done this kind of thing before," Matthew said quietly. By 'this' he meant courting. Going out with someone without the intention of sleeping with them at that very moment or extremely soon. Hell, he never even met people under the guise of wishing to court. It was practically a foreign word to him.

"There is a first time for everything," Thursday answered.

Matthew looked back to Finn. There was a tug in his gut. Like some sort of invisible force was trying to drag him over to the healer.

"Go on," Thursday's voice floated in his ear. "Live a little."

"I live a lot," Matthew answered.

"Not like this." Thursday gave Matthew's lower back an encouraging push. "Go catch those feelings."

Matthew turned to look at Thursday. She stood there, her arms full of dirty dishes and with a silly smile on her face. It was a genuine smile, not the snide or sarcastic smirks that she wore when she had some sort of hidden agenda.

"Thank you," Matthew smiled.

"Go on," she repeated. "Before I change my mind about these dishes."

CHAPTER ELEVEN

Finn's head snapped up as soon as Matthew approached the table like he had sensed him coming closer. "I'm just tidying away the cards," he explained like he had to justify his actions.

"Would you like to take a break from that and come on a walk with me?" Matthew asked. He inwardly cringed at himself. He wasn't his usual smooth-talking self. He was clunky and awkward. Hopefully, he came off more confident than he felt.

Finn seemed surprised by this question. "Oh, sure," he answered. He put the cards down and made for the kitchen door.

Matthew quickly grabbed the healer's elbow to stop him. "We need to take the back door," he explained.

The air was crisp outside. The ugly clouds that had lashed the ground with rain seemed to have vanished, allowing the pink evening sky to peek through. There was still enough light to make the water on the grass glitter like there were jewels scattered across the garden.

"I always have to go out the back entrance," Matthew explained as they walked down the gravelly incline towards the back gates. "Too many people frequent the streets at the front of the house. I can't risk being seen."

"That must be difficult," Finn replied. He inhaled a giant lungful of fresh air, a look of pure bliss consuming his face. Matthew wondered how long it had been since Finn had breathed in some decent air.

"I'm used to it by this point," Matthew shrugged. "I have my ways and means of getting around without my ability getting in the way."

"Do you go out often?" Finn enquired curiously.

"Ah…"

Matthew went out often, but not in the way Finn most likely meant. The only time Matthew had ever felt like he had reason to go out was when he was seeking out comfort from another. He knew that Sybil disapproved; she didn't want him going out at all until he had mastered his ability. Now that he remembered this, it occurred to him that that was probably one of the many reasons that Thursday had encouraged this so avidly.

"…Sort of?" Matthew eventually concluded.

Finn folded his arms across his chest, bracing himself against the chill. "Sawyer did say that the only time you go out is to bed people," he said. "I didn't know whether to believe him or not."

Matthew felt dread scrape his chest. Of course, Sawyer had said something. He always stuck his nose in where it didn't belong.

"Not that I would be offended by that," Finn quickly said, worried by Matthew's lack of response. "I'm a very modern man. If it is between two consenting adults, I don't see what the problem is."

"You're not bothered by the fact that I have bedded many people?" Matthew asked, unconvinced.

Finn shrugged. "It's not my place to judge," he replied. "It's harmless."

Matthew was going to have to ask Finn to warn him any time he was going to say something surprising because the number of shocks he was getting from this one man was becoming quite ridiculous.

"Many would disagree with you on that," Matthew pointed out.

"Many do not dictate my beliefs," Finn replied.

It was as they were descending the final few metres of the path that Matthew realised that Finn was still hobbling. He felt incredibly stupid. They had walked this whole way and he had completely forgotten about Finn's injury.

"Lean on me," Matthew said, taking Finn's free hand and putting it on his upper arm. "I completely forgot about you being hurt."

"Don't be silly," Finn answered. Despite this response, Matthew still felt a significant amount of weight being pressed onto him. He hoped that Finn wasn't in too much pain.

As they reached the back gates, they came across one of Whitney's flower beds. Finn paused to examine them. This bed was covered in hydrangeas of varying colour, another splodge of iridescence amongst an otherwise sea of green.

"She is extremely deft with her hands," Finn mused.

Matthew had never thought of it that way before. "Yes, she is," he agreed. He was tempted to lean closer to see if Finn was still wearing violet water, but he restrained himself on the grounds of how creepy it would look. "She cooks; she gardens; she can set a whole building on fire with her fingertips…Pretty much a triple threat."

"Any man would be lucky to have her," Finn concluded.

This caused a surge of jealousy to fill Matthew like poison. It was completely unwarranted because he knew what Finn was attracted to, and he was positive that Whitney was not his type at all. Envy was a cruel mistress. It didn't have to make any sense or remain within the lines of logic. It struck whenever it pleased.

"Come, the gate is this way," Matthew instructed, guiding Finn away from the flower beds.

The gates that surrounded Sybil's grounds loomed over them like intimidating giants. When standing directly below them, one would almost believe that they reached into the heavens.

Matthew always kept a key to the gates on his person just in case he ever had to make a quick escape. The rusted metal bars were the only true signature of the actual age of Sybil's property, besides the old sheets thrown over furniture in many unused rooms. They used to be extremely stiff as no one went out the back way, but as Matthew began to frequent this exit, they got easier to drag open each time.

"Where does this lead out to?" Finn asked as Matthew unlocked the gates.

"An alley usually used by prostitutes and dealers," Matthew explained. The lock clicked open, and he dragged the gate out until there was enough space for them to pass through.

"Are you not concerned about these prostitutes and dealers seeing you?" Finn continued as they passed through together.

Matthew grunted as he dragged the gate shut again. It rattled and grunted back at him in protest. "They won't be here at this time of the day," he explained. "The prostitutes work the local drinking holes until nightfall and the dealers cannot let themselves be seen until their faces can be shaded by the cover of darkness."

"It is nightfall soon," Finn pointed out, gesturing to the pink sky.

Matthew shrugged. "We shall cross that bridge when we come to it."

The alley was atrocious. It was coated in grime. Muddy water bubbled out of clogged-up drains; cardboard boxes were turning to mulch against the walls; dirt was slathered across every inch of the ground. A smell Matthew dared not to guess the source of burned his nostrils like acid.

"This is the scenic route," he joked, looping his arm through Finn's once more.

"Clearly," Finn chuckled. He didn't look at all put off by their surroundings.

"I think this is one of the reasons Sybil is allowed to keep the mansion," Matthew explained. "How could anyone sell a house with such a revolting place literally on its doorstep?"

"Do such things matter?" Finn frowned.

"To rich elites, it does," Matthew sighed. A rat scampered across their path. "We'd have more of those sniffing around Sybil's garden if it wasn't for Crissy's cat."

"Crissy?"

"Christine. She's a prostitute who works the alley most of the week. Her husband bought her a cat called Radley. Excellent mouser, thank God," Matthew explained. Finn had this baffled expression on his face and Matthew didn't understand what had confused him so. "What?"

"A prostitute with a husband?" Finn asked incredulously.

"Oh, yes," Matthew replied, a cheeky grin tugging at the corners of his mouth. "Christine and Nathanial are both prostitutes. Nathanial works the streets closer to Adelia Day's establishment, though. They're both very good at what they do."

Finn looked completely flabbergasted. "And you would know this by experience?"

Matthew pressed his lips together dumbly, silent for a moment. "Maybe," he finally answered.

To his surprise, Finn started laughing. "You never cease to surprise me, Matthew," the healer chuckled.

"I'm glad that we're both having similar experiences with each other, then," Matthew grinned.

They continued down the alley, Matthew telling more stories of hijinks with the many colourful characters he had met there. He had never felt comfortable telling these stories to anyone but Thursday. He knew that Sybil disapproved of any type of careless behaviour; Titus always turned it into a lecture;

Whitney was disinterested in just about anything anyone had to say; and Matthew would rather turn himself inside out than talk to Sawyer about it.

Finn made him feel relaxed like there was nothing at all to be ashamed of. Maybe there wasn't. Maybe the attitudes of everyone else were what needed fixing. That would mean that Thursday made more sense than most of common society. Now *that* was a terrifying concept.

"You're joking!" Finn laughed.

"I am not! I am in bed with this woman and suddenly she tells me that she has another man coming around to join us. Here I am, looking like a six-foot-tall muscled alpha male and she has a *man* coming around. How in the name of sanity could I explain myself if I turned into some dainty female before her very eyes?" Matthew exclaimed.

"What did you do, then?" Finn's eyes were wide and glistening, hooked on every word Matthew said.

"I got the hell out of there!" Matthew answered. "I told her I wasn't into that sort of thing, and I ran for my life!"

Finn was in stitches, having to lean against Matthew more than he intended to so that he could keep his footing. Matthew admired the healer's laughing face, a content smile on his own as he watched. "Imagine if you had stayed and didn't change at all when the man arrived," Finn said breathlessly.

"Now *that* would have been a plot twist," Matthew laughed.

They both stood there for a moment, snickering to themselves like little children. Matthew glanced up at the sky and his heart sank as he realised how dark it had gotten. It felt like they had only been walking through the alley for five minutes, how had it gotten so dark so quickly?

Finn looked up, too. "It's getting dark," he unhelpfully pointed out.

"This place will soon be full of people," Matthew reluctantly sighed. "We should probably head back."

Seeing the reluctance on Matthew's face, Finn started looking around himself. Matthew watched the other man with a curious but baffled expression on his face. He looked like he had suddenly remembered that he had lost something. "What in the world are you doing?" Matthew asked.

"Ah-ha!" Finn raced forward a couple of metres; his run was undoubtedly hilarious due to his injury. Matthew followed, unsure what was going on but more than willing to follow.

Finn pointed at an abandoned ladder before grabbing it and dragging it up against a nearby building. It ended just short of the rooftop but the gap between the top of the ladder and the roof itself was not large.

"Let's go up there," Finn said excitedly. "You can't even see the top of the roof from down here. We would be hidden from sight."

Matthew was all for spontaneity and risk, but he couldn't help looking at Finn's cane. "Would you be able to climb in your state?" he asked.

Finn raised his eyebrows. "My state?" he repeated. "My state is just fine, thank you very much. I wouldn't suggest the idea if I didn't believe myself capable of it. Come!" Finn proceeded to jam his cane between his teeth and began to climb the ladder.

He was absolutely mad.

Matthew loved it.

When there was enough space between them, Matthew started to climb the ladder. He forced himself to be a gentleman and keep his eyes focused straight in front of him instead of straying upwards to his ascending companion.

Being a gentleman was hard.

Matthew slung himself up onto the roof and joined Finn near the edge. They looked down at the dark alley below as people began to filter in. Sketchy men in long coats and women caked in makeup claiming their spots for the night. Matthew even thought that he saw Christine walking past carrying Radley in her arms.

"It's amazing how resilient human beings are," Finn commented.

Matthew quirked an eyebrow. "What do you mean?" he asked, his eyes following Christine's journey until she disappeared from their view.

"These people are clearly in a difficult situation, most likely financially," Finn explained. "Instead of giving up, here they are. Doing whatever they can to keep living. It's rather beautiful."

"You find prostitution beautiful?" Matthew scoffed. He believed even the prostitutes themselves would disagree on the matter. Especially those who didn't meet their quotas and suffered the consequences.

Finn rolled his eyes. "I find a prostitute's determination to live beautiful."

Matthew had always just viewed prostitution as a desperate means of earning money. What Finn described made sense, though. A lot of the men and women Matthew had slept with from this very alley were headstrong and assertive. They lived beautifully traumatic lives. If only the rest of the world saw it that way.

"You say the strangest things," Matthew commented. "Pretentious as hell, but strange all the same."

"The smile on your face makes me think that this isn't entirely a bad thing?" Finn asked.

Matthew's grin widened. "No, I actually find it rather endearing."

He looked at Finn. Despite the healer not looking in his direction, Matthew could still see the tiny smile that Finn was trying to force down. Matthew tried not to chuckle. He knew all about the 'trying to stay disinterested' act. It was a ploy commonly used by novices who didn't want to scare the other person away by seeming too emotional or invested. He had witnessed it a lot at Adelia Day's and other molly houses.

He didn't know a way to tell Finn that there was nothing he could do at this point that would scare him away.

They sat down on the rooftop, hidden from view by the dark of the night. Matthew let his head rest against the wall, so he could stare up at the sky. The stars were so tiny, yet so bright, Matthew wondered how far they were from where he currently sat.

"My mother used to tell me that the stars were sky fairies," Finn mused like he had read Matthew's mind.

Matthew scoffed lightly. "The kids at the orphanage said the stars were Satan's minions sent to make us sin," he replied. He felt Finn's eyes on him, and he shifted uncomfortably. He chuckled, trying to make light of what he had said. "But then again, that could have been just what they said to me."

"You lived in an orphanage?" Finn asked. His voice was quiet and gentle. "If you don't mind my asking, of course."

"Yes, I did," Matthew answered, wanting to assure Finn that he wasn't intruding by asking the question. "It was in the Davidson District of Opara City. I think I was born there. I can't know for sure."

"I'm assuming it was a religious establishment if the kids were thinking of sin and Satan," Finn replied.

Matthew nodded. "It was run by the nuns of the Church of Immaculate Conception," he answered. He pulled a face. "I hated those nuns."

"What happened to your parents?" Finn asked softly, before quickly adding, "You don't have to answer that if you don't want to."

"Sister Diana always made sure that I knew that I was abandoned for being the spawn of the devil," Matthew shrugged, trying to make it sound like no big deal. "She told me I was lucky that Father Howard took me in. *If I had my way, you would have been drowned in the nearest well,*' was what she always said."

Finn made a disgusted noise at the back of his throat. "What a horrible woman," he said.

"I don't blame her." Matthew let his head roll to the right, his eyes falling on Finn's outline in the darkness. "I shifted as a child. Can you imagine how terrifying that was for her? For the kids at the orphanage? Thankfully, the whole 'the person you desire most' rubbish came later. As a kid, my eyes just changed, and sometimes my hair and skin tone did too. Still, it was enough to terrify them. I was lucky they didn't throw me into United Arms or, as Sister Diana said, drowned me in a well."

"Don't say stupid things like that," Finn scolded. "You were a child, just like any other. Just because you were a little different did not mean you deserved such horrible treatment."

Matthew shrugged. Thursday had been less eloquent about her disgust with Sister Diana and her band of nuns, and he had to beg her not to burn the place down. As much as he had despised the place, The Church of Immaculate Conception had saved a lot of children in the Davidson District and beyond. *Normal* children. Children who weren't believed to be spawns of the devil or a witch's minion.

"What about you?" he asked Finn, wanting desperately to change the subject. Sister Diana; Father Howard; those kids… All of that was behind him. It was his past, and he wanted it to stay there. "Were you raised in the Circus?"

It was Finn's turn to look at the sky. Matthew examined the healer's shadowed profile, from the arch of his browbone, across the cut of his jaw and the slope of his nose. Finn had a tiny bump at the top of his nose where his bone seemed to jut out the tiniest of bits. This little imperfection somehow made the healer more attractive. Matthew resisted the temptation to reach across and brush his thumb along it.

"No," Finn eventually said, his voice shaking Matthew from his admiration. "I lived on the streets with my mother for a very long time before the circus."

Matthew turned onto his side so that he could watch Finn more easily. He could sense unease in Finn's voice. "Is she…" he didn't know how to finish the sentence without sounding invasive.

"Yeah," Finn quietly replied. "I presume so."

"You presume so?" Matthew echoed.

Finn coughed nervously. "My Mum was different. Not like us, but in another way. She… saw things differently. She always talked about seeing different colours when she heard certain sounds. I remember her even mentioning to me about numbers and letters having genders and assigned colours. It didn't bother or hinder her in any way… I just wish I knew what it had been that made her like that."

Matthew had never heard of such a condition before. "You couldn't… heal it?" he asked.

"My ability does not stretch to the ailments of the mind," Finn answered. "I never found out what plagued her before she was taken."

A lump formed in Matthew's throat. "Taken?"

"Ah, yeah," Finn answered, his voice shaking at the end of the sentence. "One of the men who took shelter near us told a warden of United Arms about my mother. I don't know if you remember, but there was a time when the asylum was offering money for people to tip them off about possible… *patients*." He spat the last word like it burned his mouth.

Matthew remembered that time well. It had been well over thirty years ago, but he could not burn the memory of Sister Frances threatening to have him admitted so that they could repair damages the church had received in a recent storm out of his mind. He could see where this was going.

"They took her while I slept," Finn muttered despondently. "The circus found me not long after. I had nowhere else to go, so I went with them."

Matthew closed his eyes briefly. Such a depraved world they lived in. Every day felt like every man for himself. Everyone was trying to survive, and if that meant throwing someone else to the dogs, they didn't think twice. He was lucky that Father Howard took pride in his generous deed of taking in the poisoned orphan, or else Sister Frances could have offered him to United Arms for money. All to fix a damn church. He and Thursday could very well have met one another in neighbouring cells.

He had been lucky. A blessing that Finn's mother had not been granted. Matthew knew that the only hope Finn had was that she had died quickly in the asylum. The alternative was unimaginable.

Matthew nudged the cane separating them out of the way and shifted closer to Finn. He didn't care if it seemed too forward or creepy, he wrapped an arm around the healer's neck.

"I'm sorry," he murmured.

Finn sniffed, trying to play it off as nothing. "It was so long ago now. I just wish I had not been so foolish as to let her talk about it so openly. I wish I had not gone with the circus. I should have gone to find her."

It was Matthew's turn to scold. "Now *you're* being stupid," he said. "You couldn't have predicted any of that."

Finn laughed but the sound was hollow. "I've never talked about this with anyone before now," he said.

Matthew smiled sadly. "I haven't either," he sympathised.

The only person who knew about how bad The Church of Mother Mary had been was Thursday, and that was only because she had found Matthew there. As unreliable as Thursday could sometimes be, she was fiercely loyal when it came to Matthew's secrets. He didn't know why she favoured him, but he felt like it had something to do with how her own family had treated her.

"There's something about you," Finn said. "I'm always drawn back to you. I feel safe spilling my secrets like it's nothing to you."

"Maybe it's because I'm your *perfect beauty*," Matthew joked, attempting to lighten the mood.

Finn chuckled, his head instinctively falling onto Matthew's shoulder. Matthew's heart exploded inside his chest, and he held his breath for a moment. It felt as if breathing out, and the slight shift it would cause his body was going to scare Finn back.

A moment later, he relaxed and let his head rest gently against Finn's mane of soft hair.

Matthew could smell violet water.

"Could be," Finn conceded.

"So, you admit it?" Matthew accused, grinning.

Matthew didn't have to see Finn's face clearly to know that he was blushing. "I figured it was pretty obvious," he said. "One cannot exactly hide one's desires from you, can they?"

"Yet I still find you such a fascinating enigma," Matthew mused thoughtfully.

Finn snorted with amusement. Immediately, he covered his mouth and nose in horror.

Matthew bit his lip to fight back a smile "I also find you painfully adorable," he added.

Finn's face burned against Matthew's arm. "Well, I know you feel the same way!" he said defensively.

"I know," Matthew replied unabashedly with an easy shrug. "I told you. I find you incredibly captivating and attractive."

"Do you tell that to all the people you bed?" Finn teased.

"No, actually, I don't," Matthew admitted. "It's all purely sexual with them. I form a few friendships along the way, but I never really get to see them again after the nights we spend together, Ophelia is a special exception. You are the first person

I've been…" Matthew rolled his tongue around his mouth for a moment to find the right word, "*enamoured* by."

Finn's silence told that he was unconvinced by what Matthew was saying. Matthew could understand. Even he used to find compliments difficult to accept. After spending so long being teased and ridiculed for his ability, it was daunting to suddenly be sought after and wanted for it when he got older. Something told him that Finn had a similar experience. He had a feeling that the ringmaster of the circus wasn't the complimentary type.

"I don't think you understand how important it is to me that I didn't change," Matthew insisted. "I've never had that before. Everyone has always wanted someone else, someone who isn't me. Even my family back at Sybil's mansion couldn't help turning me into something else when they first looked at me. Everyone always wants something different. Never *me*."

Finn straightened up, watching Matthew carefully. "That's their loss," he said quietly.

"You are the first person to see me," Matthew whispered back.

They stared at each other for a moment.

Somehow, Matthew could see Finn's eyes, like the deep blue pulled away the darkness like a curtain and drilled into his very soul. Matthew wanted to get lost in them; to drown happily in them; to never stop looking at them. Such kind eyes. The eyes that defied his ability. The eyes that saw what no one else could.

Then there were lips on top of his own.

It was an act of impulse, and Matthew felt Finn immediately begin to draw back fearfully. He didn't let that happen. He took the healer's face in both his hands and drew him closer, making sure he knew that it was okay. More than okay.

Matthew's heart swelled like a balloon. His senses were singing, awoken by the kiss that he had been unwittingly waiting for his entire life. It felt like, somehow, everything had been leading up to this point. Like every bedded prostitute; every rushed sexual encounter; every lecture from Titus; every eye roll from Whitney and insult from Sawyer, had all leading up to this moment.

The moment when someone would kiss him, not because of some mirage or illusion; not because they were tricked into seeing a different face; but because they saw him as he was and did not want to change him.

Finn *saw* him.

This moment was a moment of freedom; of expression; of release. This was the moment where a man who had been terrified of his desire; of what he had been born to be; of himself, acted upon his own urge, putting his own wishes and wants first for once. This was a moment of need; of passion; of emotion. A moment where the rest of society didn't matter and where their tired old beliefs were nothing but echoes in the wind as it whistled through their hair.

This moment was the first moment where Finn allowed himself to be selfish.

And Matthew was honoured to be part of that moment, for everything that it was.

Then just like that, the lips were gone, and Matthew's mouth felt cold.

"I am so sorry," Finn was immediately saying. "I don't know what came over me!"

Matthew blinked slowly, trying to process why the moment had ended so abruptly. Things slowly slid back into focus, and he saw Finn's face, inches from his own, a panicked expression embedded in his features. His mouth was moving, but Matthew couldn't hear what he was saying, deafened by the blood that was pumping through his ears.

His eyes zoned in on Finn's nose and he reached out, brushing his thumb along the bump he had noticed earlier. Finn's mouth stopped moving and he stared, his eyes wide with surprise.

"You've got a bump on your nose," Matthew murmured. He heard himself speak and, like it broke some sort of spell, his hearing roared back into life.

"Yeah," Finn said slowly, clearly confused. "I broke my nose in the circus." Matthew drifted closer as the healer spoke, his finger slipping down from Finn's nose to hold his cheek. "It was a pretty bad fracture, so it healed like this…"

It didn't matter what else Finn had to say because Matthew chose to taste the words from his lips instead.

Time always became irrelevant when wrapped in an intimate embrace. Five minutes could pass, or fifty, and the couple would never notice. Matthew had experienced this a lot in his long life, but this was the first time he found that he didn't want it to end. If handed a pocket watch right at this moment, he would crush it beneath his heel in the hopes that it would freeze the annoying ticking noise that symbolised the passing of precious time.

This was an impossible feat, even for two impossible men like themselves, and eventually, Finn broke the embrace with a gasp. Matthew couldn't suppress his grin as he realised that the healer had been holding his breath.

"There's a way of breathing through your nose that can make kissing longer," Matthew whispered like he was confiding a massive secret. "I can teach you."

Finn chuckled quietly. "That is very generous of you," he replied.

The wind brushed past them, and the smell of violet filled Matthew's nostrils. He tugged Finn close and nestled his face in his neck, absorbing the scent abashedly for the first time. It mingled with the slight whiff of perspiration, just the perfect amount of musk to create a scent that Matthew couldn't get enough of.

"Do you like violet water?" Finn asked.

Matthew hummed his approval.

The pair of them just sat like that, on top of the roof, bathed in darkness and surrounded by the smell of violet water. Matthew felt content, more relaxed than he had ever been in his entire life. It didn't matter what was going on below them, the sound of heckling dealers; catcalling clients; baying prostitutes, all of it melted into a peaceful quiet that left only one sound throbbing against Matthew's ear.

The pulsing beat of Finn's blood pumping through his veins. The most simple but eloquent confirmation of life. A life that devotes itself to saving others. A life that Matthew never realised he was thankful for existing until it came into his life.

~M~

"Oh, my goodness, I have a crick in my neck," Finn complained as they walked up the alley again the next morning.

They had not meant to fall asleep on top of the roof, but it's surprising how easily one drifts away when so comfortable. Thankfully, it had not rained, and the temperature didn't drop to anything drastic, but they both looked like they had been dragged through a hedge regardless.

"I'll give your neck a rub when we get back," Matthew grinned.

"How considerate of you," Finn replied, rolling his eyes with a smile.

"It is the least I can do to make up for when you healed me," Matthew answered.

"I have a feeling that I will have to be healing you a lot in the future," Finn commented, "so I don't think you should start trying to return favours or you'll never be done doing it."

Matthew laughed. "You underestimate my dedication, good sir."

The pair entered the grounds of Sybil's mansion through the same gate they had exited through. It was a muggy morning, the air heavy with moisture and a slight mist hanging over the grass. It gave the building a slightly sinister aura. Like the haunted houses where children were rumoured to have been murdered by their horrid fathers, left to wander the grounds forever as a ghoulish apparition.

Thankfully, the only murder that ever took place in Sybil's house had been Thursday's disastrous attempts at cooking back in the day.

It was as they drew closer to the building that Matthew realised that something was wrong. He pulled to a stop, confused. Finn halted beside him and looked at him quizzically.

"Something doesn't seem right," Matthew frowned.

"What do you mean?" Finn asked, looking up at their home in confusion.

"I don't know. Something just... it doesn't feel right."

Matthew approached the back door with care. It was when he reached it that he saw what had caused such unease.

The door was lying wide open, the glass cracked, and the hinges busted.

Someone had broken into the house.

CHAPTER TWELVE

Matthew and Finn entered the kitchen with caution. It was eerily silent. This was not normal for a house full of people. The clock read nine in the morning, at least one person would have been awake by now. Matthew felt a hard lump of fear swell in his throat as they left the kitchen into the hallway.

He didn't like this at all. Even if the house had been broken into by a thief or a murderer, his family were more than capable of taking care of it. The fact that there didn't seem to be anyone around made him feel incredibly uneasy. What could have happened? They wouldn't have just left the door hanging open like that if they had apprehended the perpetrator. They weren't that careless.

They came out into the foyer. Matthew strained to listen to any signs of life. Anything at all.

His attention was immediately grabbed by a noise coming from the door behind the stairs. Voices. Voices in the basement.

Finn grabbed his wrist when he moved toward the sound.

"What if it's dangerous?" the healer hissed.

"They're my family, I have to help them," Matthew answered. "Hell, for all we know they're just having a séance down there. Sacrificing Titus to his God in exchange for three wishes."

Finn shook his head. "I know you don't believe that."

Matthew sighed. "No, I don't. They wouldn't leave the door hanging open like that, so whoever has broken in is down there. Most likely with them. They aren't easy people to outwit, meaning whoever this is could be just as dangerous as we are. I must do something."

"And you think walking in without a plan is going to be at all beneficial?" Finn exclaimed.

Matthew shrugged, forcing a smile. "It's what I do best." He saw the grave look on Finn's face and sighed. "Look, you stay here. This person could be armed. They could be like us; they could be dangerous."

Finn's blue eyes darkened. "I'm not going to just sit here!" he said firmly. "I'm coming with you."

Matthew snatched the hand that was gripping his wrist and pulled Finn closer so that he could see how serious he was. "You can't heal, Finn. You'd be extremely vulnerable," Matthew growled. "You have to stay here."

"You can't heal either," Finn threw back, in a gravelly voice of his own. "I must be there in case you get hurt. Now stop wasting time bickering with me, we need to help our family."

They were nose to nose. Both were scowling, both not appreciating being told what to do. Matthew could see that Finn was not going to change his mind, and the longer they stood there arguing, the longer their family could be in danger.

Matthew sighed heavily. "Fine but stay behind me."

Matthew didn't go into the basement often. This was mainly because he didn't have a reason to go down there. What use did he have for a cluttered, dark room full of dust and hordes of spiders? It had nothing to do with the fact that he was claustrophobic and hated the thought of being underground. Of course not.

He had to suck it up now, for the closer they got to the door, the clearer the distress in the voices became. He could distinctly make out Thursday, her voice always unmistakable. It was hard to make out what exactly she was saying, but Matthew could recognise the tones and lilts of her voice through sheet metal.

Easing the door open as gently as he could, Matthew remembered something important: They had been holding Charles down in the basement until Sybil returned. Maybe more of his friends had come to help him escape? But surely, they would have been easily dealt with? None of this made any sense.

His heart was in his throat as they crept down the old, creaky stairs. Matthew was afraid they would draw attention to themselves. The only thing they had going for themselves now was the element of surprise. Matthew wasn't sure what exactly they were going to do with that element of surprise, but he was hoping that inspiration would strike him down any moment now.

There was a lot of clutter in the basement, most of it packed away into tall towers of boxes that stretched up to the ceiling. Matthew crept around each box mountain, keeping himself hidden from view. He relied on Finn to do the same as he followed him.

The voices were now discernible, and Matthew listened as he and Finn got closer and closer to the source.

". . . rather boring. Sybil will be back soon, and then you'll be in trouble."

"Do you think I'm frightened by the prospect of jail? Of the hangman's noose? I've been threatened by it before, and I have slipped my way out."

"You seem like the slimy sort."

"Your insults won't work on me."

"They're not for you, they're for me."

Thursday was the first person Matthew saw. She was sitting against a wall of boxes, her hands behind her back. She didn't look to be distressed, but with Thursday one could never gauge the severity of a situation purely by the look on her face. Titus sat on one side of her, and Sawyer sat on the opposite side.

Then, standing in front of them with her back to Matthew, was… Ophelia?

She was holding a knife to Charles, who was still bound to the chair they had left him in.

Whitney was nowhere to be seen.

Thursday was doing most of the talking, which wasn't surprising. "You're almost as unhinged as I am," she said. "He won't thank you for this, you know. He'll resent you for it."

"You can't know that," Ophelia replied.

Thursday's eyebrows shot up her head. "Are you insane? I know him more than you do. We're his family, for the love of God. What am I talking about? You *are* insane."

"Family?" Ophelia scoffed. "He doesn't need family. He only needs me."

Matthew couldn't understand what was happening. Why was Ophelia holding her husband at knifepoint while raving about their love? It didn't make any sense. But Charles wasn't Thursday's family. What on earth was Ophelia doing? Why weren't the others trying to stop her?

"Now I know why I didn't like you," Thursday hissed. "You remind me of the Asylum!"

"Matthew and I will be together forever; all we need to do is get you out of the way!" Ophelia declared. "All of you! You're nothing but obstacles!"

"What?"

Matthew's heart leapt into his throat as the word left his mouth. He slapped his hand over his lips in horror and hid behind the boxes again. He couldn't breathe. What was Ophelia talking about? Matthew had thought that he had made it clear to her that they couldn't be together in that way. Maybe she hadn't understood him? But then why was she holding Charles at knifepoint? Why was she fighting with Thursday?

"Matthew?" Ophelia frowned, looking around. Her heels clicked against the ground as she walked toward them, each step hitting Matthew in the chest like a punch.

Taking a deep breath, Matthew lunged out at her. He tried to wrestle the knife from her hand in her moment of surprise, but Ophelia must have been expecting him. She lashed out with a scream, clearly inexperienced with using a knife as a weapon.

Hot pain slashed across Matthew's arm, and he stumbled back. He grabbed his bicep, despite himself.

"You stay right there!" Ophelia screamed at Finn, pointing her knife at him when he tried to go to heal Matthew. He froze, his eyes flickering between the blade dripping in blood and the wound on Matthew's arm. He didn't yet know that physical wounds didn't appear on Matthew's body. Relief from the shooting pain the blade caused wouldn't have gone amiss, though.

"Ophelia, what the hell are you doing?" Matthew barked.

Ophelia turned to Matthew, her face immediately softening as she gazed at him. "I'm doing this for us," she explained. "So that we can be together."

"I already told you that I wasn't interested in being with you in that way!" Matthew exclaimed.

"I figured that was because I'm married," Ophelia explained, her eyes wide. "I took my husband out of the equation so you would change your mind!"

Matthew's eyes fell on Charles. His breath caught in his throat when he saw that the man's neck had been slit. His head was drooped, and his skin was pale.

"Ophelia, you didn't…" Matthew trailed off, unable to find words.

"It turns out that Ophelia here has a history of instability," Thursday spoke up, folding her arms. Wait, she wasn't bound up? "Charles isn't even her husband."

Matthew couldn't believe what he was hearing. This had to be lies. Ophelia wasn't unstable! She was perfectly sound, just like any other woman her age!

"How did you find this out?" Matthew asked incredulously.

"They invaded my privacy!" Ophelia yelled, pointing the knife threateningly at Thursday and Sawyer.

Sawyer, not at all threatened by the knife in his face, sighed and pointed out, "All I did was investigate her history. I just wanted to make sure that she was who she claimed to be. I didn't want Sybil to offer our home to a filthy, lying human. I found her family tree and visited her ailing sister. She was more than willing to talk." Sawyer smirked darkly. "Just my luck, right?"

Matthew wanted to scream at Sawyer. Why had he been so invasive? Why could he never just let things be? But, if he hadn't, they wouldn't have discovered this important detail about Ophelia's life.

"As soon as Sawyer confronted her, she went crazy," Thursday said, rolling her eyes. "She kicked the back door in and started swinging that knife around. When we discovered Charles' body, she started threatening to take her own life. We've been trying to talk her down ever since."

"We couldn't save Charles," Titus quickly added. "She killed him sometime yesterday."

"When?" Matthew demanded, looking at Ophelia desperately. "When did you kill him?"

Ophelia tilted her head and pursed her lips. "I did it when you told me you didn't want to court me. It was because of him, wasn't it? Well, he's not in the way anymore. We can be together now!"

Matthew stared at Charles' dead body in disbelief. He couldn't wrap his mind around what he was being told. Ophelia had seemed so understanding and sane when Matthew had told her that a relationship between them wouldn't work. They moved on from the topic so quickly, that he thought that it hadn't meant that much to her. He had thought it had just been a fleeting question; a fleeting hope; a wish of minuscule importance. Yet this man was dead because of him. Ophelia had somehow gotten it into her head that murdering her husband would improve her chances of getting to be with Matthew.

"I don't... I can't... Ophelia, you murdered Charles," Matthew stammered. "Whatever possibility, however small, there had been for us to have a chance died with Charles."

"You don't know what you're talking about," Ophelia laughed. "Don't you see? Charles isn't in the way of us anymore."

"There isn't an 'us'!" Matthew exclaimed.

"Not yet!" Ophelia insisted.

"No, *never.*"

Ophelia narrowed her eyes. She lifted her arm, a severe glint in her eyes, and pointed the knife at Finn. "Is it because of him?" she growled.

Matthew and Finn exchanged a look of alarm. Finn didn't look scared, but Matthew sure as hell was. That knife could easily end his life. End it before it had even really started.

Thursday slowly rose to her feet. "Don't be stupid," she snapped. "I was fine to sit here and let you rave about ending your own sorry life, but once you threaten one of my own, that's when I start getting annoyed."

"One of your own," Ophelia repeated mockingly.

"Ophelia," Titus said gently, also rising from the ground, "think of what the Lord would think."

"The Lord abandoned me!" Ophelia barked at him.

"The Lord never abandons," Titus answered sternly.

Ophelia's arm shook with rage. She inched over to Finn, the knife trembling with the rest of her body. Matthew tried to step closer to them, but Ophelia lashed out again, swinging her arm wildly around her body so that the blade cut through the air in various directions. Finn had to jump back to avoid being sliced, and that was enough to get Matthew to stop moving. Even Thursday paused mid-step.

Ophelia truly was unstable.

Unstable and armed. Not a good combination.

"If you are in the way, you will go too," Ophelia hissed.

"I am not in anyone's way," Finn answered calmly. He didn't so much as flinch when Ophelia came face to face with him. "I do believe in free will, though. Matthew deserves the right to court whoever he wants, regardless of their, uh, body count. Or their impractical methods of getting one's attention."

Matthew's heart was pounding in his chest. He couldn't breathe. It would only take one swipe of Ophelia's arm and she could cut Finn's throat wide open. Why wasn't he afraid? Why wasn't he scared? He ached to lunge at Ophelia and drag her away, but he feared that he wouldn't be fast enough.

"I would be careful of who you call impractical," Ophelia snarled. "I'm the one with the knife."

"Yes, believe me, I have noticed," Finn answered. Despite saying this, his eyes weren't on the weapon in question. They were trained on Ophelia's face. "I am painfully aware of that fact."

"Let me have him!" Ophelia screamed right into Finn's face. Finn winced and leaned back slightly. "We are made for each other!"

"Do you even know him?" Finn suddenly barked back at her. "From what I understand, you fell for a Spanish man named Samuel! You fell for a face that isn't even his! A smile that isn't his! A voice that isn't his! You don't know Matthew; you only know Samuel! You only know the person that you want to see! Of course, you're perfect for him because Samuel was tailored for *you*!"

Ophelia didn't say anything. She glared at Finn with her lips sealed shut. Matthew didn't know what to say, the healer's outburst had come so suddenly, that he had not expected it.

"You are only clinging to him now that you know that Samuel isn't real. Do you think that I will allow Matthew to settle for being a second choice? Just because his ability dictates what people see does not mean that he must settle for being someone's afterthought! He is not someone you settle for, you insane woman! He is a man you want to be with, not because he isn't your perfect vision but is kind of alright anyway, but because you can see the caring, genuine man that he is!"

Finn and Ophelia stared each other down. Finn was panting from his rant, his face twisted with rage and passion.

Tears prickled in Matthew's eyes. No one had spoken about him in that way before. No one had ever defended his honour. Defended his right to be a person, not a face to a desire. No one had ever wanted to. He was speechless; blown away; amazed. It made all those years of torment and loneliness feel like it was worth it because it had brought him to this moment. To this incredible man. This incredible man who stared down a knife with brazen eyes and no fear. This incredible man who saw Matthew. Not Samuel; or Alina; or Maureen; or Leonard; or one of the many other faces that Matthew had taken on over the years.

Ophelia screamed and took a swing at Finn with her knife.

Matthew acted the instant he saw her hand lift. He rammed his body into Ophelia, sending them both tumbling to the floor. The knife flew from Ophelia's hand, skittering away from the entangled pair.

Matthew tried to get up again, desperate to retrieve the knife before Ophelia did. She predicted this, though, and grabbed his wrist, clamping down to make sure he didn't get far. Matthew tried to use this leverage against her, attempting to drag her with him. When she realised what he was doing, Ophelia's face soured, and she tore her hand away from him, effectively ripping her sleeve in the process.

Ophelia ripped herself away, slapping her hand over her forearm like she had been scratched.

It was too late.

They had seen it.

"Why do you have the United Arms brand?" Thursday demanded.

"I don't," Ophelia weakly protested, her fingers turning white from clutching so hard.

She couldn't deny it, though. Matthew knew what he had seen. Burned into her pale skin had been the United Arms Sigel, a mark every patient was given upon admission to the asylum. Thursday even had the Sigel once upon a time.

"Were you admitted to United Arms?" Titus asked.

"I would believe it," Sawyer muttered. He was the only one still sitting. "She's bloody insane!"

"Sawyer stop it!" Titus snapped.

"She came down here and murdered Charles as a love letter to Matthew!" Sawyer laughed. "Do not tell me that you believe that those are the actions of a sane woman!"

"I am as sane as you are!" Ophelia barked back.

Sawyer threw his hands in the air. "You see? She agrees with me!"

Thursday approached Ophelia with a hardened expression on her face. She grabbed the woman's arm and roughly yanked her to her feet. Matthew took a step forward, instinctively worried about Ophelia's safety. His confusion over what was happening caused him to draw back and observe.

"When were you released?" Thursday demanded to know. "When?!"

Ophelia scowled and yanked her arm away from Thursday. She remained silent out of… defiance? Resentment? That stubborn flare that had once attracted Matthew but in this moment chilled him to his core? He couldn't tell. There was something in Thursday's eyes that he couldn't place. What had she figured out?

"*Were* you released?" Thursday asked slowly.

"What are you suggesting?" Matthew exclaimed.

Thursday raised her eyebrows at Ophelia, who remained silent. Matthew could only see Thursday's face; he was staring at the back of Ophelia's head, so he couldn't see her expression.

"Shall I explain, then?" Thursday didn't wait for an answer. Looking over Ophelia's head at Matthew, she said, "That brand is at least a decade old."

"And? I was released," Ophelia finally protested.

Thursday did not look remotely amused. "You don't get released from United Arms. Either you die there, or you escape."

"As if you know," Ophelia hissed.

Thursday lifted her arm, the damage from where she had sliced off her brand forever visible on her skin. "I do trust me."

"So, you understand?" Ophelia's voice had lifted with excitement.

"Ophelia?" Matthew frowned.

He remembered seeing the brand on Ophelia's arm, but it was just numbers. He didn't want to ask about it, and he hadn't known what the Sigel looked like. Thursday's immediate recognition of the mark was what made him realise what it was.

At the sound of his voice, Ophelia whirled around, a manic look in her eyes. She looked so different; so unhinged; so, unlike the woman Matthew had thought he had known.

"I'm not crazy, Matthew!" she quickly insisted. "It's a... it's all a mistake!"

"Stop trying to deny it!" Thursday snapped. "I know crazy when I see it. Are you so desperate for Matthew that you will pretend to be sane?"

Ophelia rolled her eyes. "Men don't like insane women."

"Ophelia," Finn spoke up for the first time in a while. Ophelia glared at him angrily, but he didn't so much as flinch under her spiteful gaze. "Who exactly is Charles, if not your husband?"

Sawyer's hand shot into the air. He had the air of a child sitting in on a fascinating lesson in school. "I can answer that!" he declared. "I figured it was obvious."

"Clearly not," Matthew snapped.

Sawyer sighed. "Charles works for the police. Ophelia escaped from United Arms Asylum." He waited, hoping that the others would catch up. When they didn't, he gave them a reprimanding look. "Charles helped her escape from the Asylum, attempting to pass her off as his wife to everyone in his life. He most likely realised that he had made a big mistake when she started acting out and thus tried to readmit her. Which resulted in the cat and mouse game that led to our mansion yesterday morning."

"Impossible. Surely, once they discovered Ophelia was here, they would have gone through the proper process of obtaining her instead of breaking in as they did," Titus rebuked.

Sawyer raised his eyebrows. "Would you tell the people you worked with that you allowed a mental patient to escape? They were working outside the law to get her back before she did anything stupid."

Matthew thought about the men he had killed. If this was true, he had killed two people whose only crime had been breaking into the mansion. The mere thought made him feel sick.

"Is this true, Ophelia?" Matthew asked.

"I'm right, aren't I?" Sawyer grinned when Ophelia didn't answer. She gave him a dirty look, to which he responded with a dark wink.

Ophelia clenched her jaw, very clearly irritated, and rolled her eyes. "The silly man was infatuated with me. I did what any person in my situation would do and used that to my advantage. I stayed with him for about a year before I decided it was time for me to move on. He wasn't happy with this decision. So, I ran from him."

She spun on her heel to face Matthew again, her eyes twinkling.

"You see? I never loved him! We were never married! We can be together now, Matthew!" she explained. "Isn't that great?"

Matthew didn't know what he looked like externally, but internally he was drowning in disgust. He couldn't even look at the joyous expression on her face without feeling an urge to gag. He retrieved the knife from the floor and started for the door. There was nothing more he wanted right now than to be alone.

"Matthew?" Ophelia's voice had gone quiet. A moment later, it shot to a roar. "Matthew!"

The sound of heels rushing up behind him. Matthew spun around again, making Ophelia stumble to a halt by pointing the knife at her. "Don't you dare," he threatened. He walked forward, forcing Ophelia to stagger backwards. "Someone untie Charles from that chair."

Finn immediately started untying Charles. While he did this, Ophelia stared at Matthew with a desperate gaze.

"Don't you feel what I feel?" she pleaded.

"What do you know of me, truly?" Matthew threw back. "What do you know of me, Matthew, not Samuel? You don't know me. What is there to feel?"

"I know enough about you," Ophelia insisted.

Matthew inhaled, trying to keep his emotions bottled. "If you knew me, you would know that I would not thank you for killing people." His nose wrinkled against his control. "I can't feel anything but disgust for you, now."

"You don't mean that."

"Stop telling me what I do and don't feel!" Matthew screamed at her.

Ophelia flinched.

Finn handled Charles' body with care and, with the help of Titus, removed him from the basement. Thursday shoved Ophelia into the chair and started tying her to it in replacement.

The desperate look in her eyes remained but the fight had vanished. "Who else is in the way?" she pleaded to know.

Matthew rubbed his eyebrow with his knife hand, wanting nothing more than to curl up in a corner and never be acknowledged again. "No one. You're nothing to me," he stated.

Thursday slid the knife from Matthew's hand and lightly touched his arm. "We'll figure out what to do with her when Sybil gets back."

Sawyer made a point of adding, "I would take care of her myself if I didn't know it would displease my partner so."

Ignoring Sawyer, Thursday said, "For now, go and get some sleep. You look like you need it."

Matthew nodded and exited the basement. It felt like someone else was controlling his body as he drifted up the stairs to his room. He didn't feel anything. He felt empty. People were dead because of him and his stupid ability. Actual people who had families and personalities and lives of their own. Gone. Snuffed out. No more. All because he got into Ophelia's bed.

Matthew buried himself under his bedcovers, with no intention of getting up for the rest of his life.

CHAPTER THIRTEEN

MATTHEW DIDN'T SLEEP.

He didn't know how much time passed as he lay in the darkness beneath his sheets. All he did was stare into the blackness of his cocoon and think of nothing. He didn't register anything, not even the blinking of his own eyes. Matthew had completely disassociated himself, and that's the way he wanted it to stay.

There was no way for him to have known how many hours had ticked by before he was interrupted. It felt like days had passed, but he didn't care. What did it matter? He was going to stay here, under his covers, where he wasn't harming anyone or anything.

A hand touched his back on top of his quilt. It took Matthew time to realise it was there at all. Like a kite slowly drifting to the ground as the wind turned to a breeze, he was pulled back into reality. Matthew scrunched his face in irritation.

"I want to be left alone," he spat.

"I know."

Matthew closed his eyes. "I would not blame you if you told me that you no longer wished to proceed with our intimacy," he said into his mattress. "All I seem to do is attract trouble and endanger the people around me."

"I have seen no evidence to support that," Finn answered.

"Look, you don't need to act like none of this was my fault," said Matthew.

Finn's hand had started moving up and down his back soothingly. Matthew tried to resist allowing it to deter him, but he couldn't stop his muscles from loosening and his being relaxing. He hadn't released that he had been so tensed up. He had thought that he had let go of his entire self when he had disassociated. Apparently not.

"I don't see how you caused Ophelia's insanity," Finn replied.

"I didn't *cause* it, but I certainly exacerbated it," was Matthew's answer.

A quiet pause. The reason Matthew knew that Finn was still there was because his hand had not left his body.

"Stop using your ability on me!" Matthew snapped. He assumed that the instant calming effect that Finn's touch had given him had something to do with his healing ability. If so, he didn't appreciate it being used to manipulate his current state.

"I am not using my ability on you," Finn plainly stated. Another pause. "None of this is your fault."

"I don't believe you."

Finn sighed. "I know you don't, but I'm going to continue to encourage the idea until the day comes when you realise its truth."

Matthew snorted derisively. "You will be waiting a long time."

"I understand that. I am patient. Isolating yourself is not the answer. I hope you come to realise this."

"Are you really not using your ability on me?" Matthew asked quietly.

"I would never use my ability to manipulate your emotions. You have every right to feel your sorrow and frustration without my interference. Besides, my ability does not reach ailments of the mind, if you remember," Finn explained. "I just don't want you to go through this alone."

"What if I told you that I wanted to go through this alone?" Matthew threw back stubbornly.

"*Do* you want to go through this alone?" Finn asked back.

Matthew felt frustrated with Finn, but at the same time, he was comforted. He was selfish in his need for human contact and company. The simple sensation of Finn's hand on his back and the whisper of the healer's gentle words against his ear made Matthew want to burst into tears. He didn't deserve it, but he couldn't refuse it, either. He wasn't strong enough.

Matthew lifted his arm, creating a space in the sheets. Finn followed the signal and climbed into Matthew's bed. He didn't lie behind him like he was expecting, though. Instead, the healer sat on the mattress and shifted the sheets away from Matthew's head.

With gentle hands, Finn captured Matthew's head between his hands, framing the shifter's face with his fingers and thumbs. As the golden light began to seep from his skin, he explained, "I am only soothing the muscles in your head. Stress like this often brings headaches along with it."

Matthew instantly felt mollified by Finn's ability. True to the healer's word, he did not even attempt to touch the shifter's emotions-if he even could-and only relax the tension in Matthew's head.

"Talk to me," Finn said gently. "It doesn't have to be about what happened. Just talk to me about anything. Anything at all."

Without the pressure to unload his emotions on Finn, Matthew felt relieved. He wasn't sure how to put his feelings into words. All he knew was that he was miserable, and he didn't want to talk about it. It felt like if he even tried to voice it then he would have to relive his sorrow, which would only worsen his current state.

"I once mistook Chrissy's cat for a rat in the alley and screamed like a complete ninny," Matthew explained, the random recollection leaving his lips before he had thought about it.

Finn chuckled. "You're afraid of rats?"

"I am not," Matthew protested. "I am, however, afraid of rats that are the size of Radley. Rats which don't exist, it seems, thank the Lord."

"Yes, the Lord certainly was careful when it came to his design of rats," Finn replied. Matthew could hear the smile in the healer's voice. "I'm sure he understood size is an important factor. That's why he made those giraffe creatures' necks so... long."

A grin threatened to tug at Matthew's lips. "Have you ever seen one of those? A giraffe, I mean?"

"Where from? My wild imaginary adventures?" Finn responded.

"Only ever seen the pictures in the books, then?" Matthew remembered seeing one of those giraffe animals once. It had been in a book in the orphanage's library. It felt like forever ago, but Matthew remembered wondering what the view was like so high up.

"The circus had an elephant," Finn added.

"Oh?" Matthew couldn't lie, he was impressed by that. The most exotic animal he had ever seen was Radley, and he only considered that cat exotic because it had one eye from a night when Nathaniel's pimp got exceptionally aggravated.

"It was not the best example of a happy animal," Finn sighed. "You know the rumours about what circuses are like, I'm sure. Well, my circus had enough animals to fill Noah's blooming ark, all of them miserable."

Noah's Ark.

"Do you think Titus would be willing to speak to me?" Matthew asked.

"I don't see why not. Why? Wanting answers on how the entire world could possibly flood all at once?" Finn asked back.

"I need advice."

Finn didn't question this. "I say you should ask him. There's no harm in that."

Matthew closed his eyes and groaned. "Titus hates me."

"I'm sure that you are very wrong," Finn answered. "I thought that the whole point of this house and this unit is that you are all a family."

"Family only tolerates each other. In special cases anyways."

"Not this kind of family."

Matthew had heard this all before from Sybil. This family was special; this family wasn't bonded by blood; they were connected through nature and experience; this family were brought together by a miracle in human biology. It was not possible for them to hate each other, no matter what it seemed like. Irritated by each other? Of course. Hatred, though? No.

Even though Matthew would trust Sybil's word to his dying day, he just couldn't believe this. If Titus didn't hate him, Sawyer certainly did. The family values idea was nice and all but put it into practice and it didn't always work out. Special family made up of miracles or not.

"Titus is a good man," Finn continued. "I've had many interesting conversations with him over the past few weeks. I think you underestimate him. He doesn't strike me as a man capable of hatred."

"Well, I tend to be a special case to these things," Matthew answered. "If he were to feel hatred, I would say that it would be towards me."

"Titus is a man of faith, correct?" Finn asked.

"Yes," Matthew sighed. "I have never seen him without that crucifix around his neck."

"Is the whole point of faith not living a life free of hatred?"

"Depends on the faith."

Finn sighed. "There's no harm in trying. You would be surprised what may come of it."

Matthew only hoped that Finn was right.

~M~

Titus was sitting perfectly straight in his chair. Matthew wondered if he was comfortable sitting as stiff as a board like that. Surely not. No one with an actual human spine could find that position comforting.

"I must say that I'm extremely confused about why you would wish to speak with me," Titus admitted, pulling Matthew from his chair-oriented thoughts.

"Why's that?" Matthew asked.

They were in Titus' room, beside the blazing fire. Matthew felt fidgety, like a child about to be scolded by their principal. This was Titus' space. An alien world for Matthew. He had expected to walk in and be overwhelmed with religious paraphernalia, but apart from a cross by his bedside table and a set of rosary beads hanging from the headboard of the bed, there wasn't anything like that. The room was covered with more paper than anything else. Scrunched up pieces on the floor; around the desk; on top of the desk; and even on the bedside table. They were full of scribbles. Mathew knew that Titus liked to write, but he never knew what it was the man wrote about.

"We don't exactly… speak," Titus answered. "Recreationally, anyway."

Matthew knew what Titus meant. The pair didn't ignore one another, but casual conversation with one another was not something that they excelled in. Matthew could talk the leg of anyone, but he could never get the hang of chatting with Titus. They didn't have enough in common to hold a talk that existed beyond swift pleasantries.

"I know," Matthew conceded. "But I feel like you would know more about this in comparison to anyone else."

Titus raised his eyebrows. "What is it that you want to know?"

Matthew sighed, feeling incredibly uncomfortable. "How do you keep your faith? Even after disasters like what happened today?"

The younger man's face turned serious. "I didn't think that you cared about my faith."

"I didn't," Matthew admitted. "Usually, I can survive on a smile and a distasteful comment, but all of that… All of that was when the disasters weren't directly linked to me. This? This is all my fault, and I don't know how to deal with it. Finn had to force me out of bed to even come down here. I'm lost. I could use a little faith right now."

Matthew expected Titus to scoff at him. To go on some sort of rant about how faith wasn't just something that you adopted when it suited you, with a bit about the sanctity of God for good measure.

Except that didn't come. The firelight flickered off the chestnut brown of Titus' irises and for once Matthew didn't feel judged under his gaze. It was softer. Kinder.

"That wasn't your fault," Titus said.

"Funny, it sounds like you meant that," Matthew replied.

Titus rolled his eyes. "I do mean it."

"Do you not think what happened with Ophelia was some sort of punishment from God for my lecherous ways?" Matthew asked dryly.

"Ophelia is responsible for Ophelia. You are not responsible for her actions," Titus explained. "The poor woman is unwell. That doesn't excuse what she did. However, you didn't know this. She had us all fooled…even me."

Matthew had forgotten that Titus and Ophelia had bonded through prayer. It was rare for Titus to have someone to discuss his religion with. Matthew had not thought of it that way until that exact moment. Titus may not have known Ophelia in the same way that Matthew had done, but he had forged a friendship of sorts with her regardless.

"How can someone with the same beliefs as you become so crazy?"

Titus chuckled. "Believing in God does not automatically make you a decent, stable person," he said. "Nowhere in *my* beliefs does it condone murder. Ophelia thinks otherwise. We all interpret things differently, I guess."

"Ophelia believed that God had abandoned her," Matthew pointed out.

"We all go through that," Titus sighed. "How we choose to cope with it defines us."

"Did you go through that?"

Titus shrugged. His face had an unreadable expression on it, although that wasn't odd for Titus.

"Many things have tested my faith," he admitted. "My time on the Sanderson's plantation; the fact that I can't go outdoors without risking my safety; the fact that women like Ophelia, and even like Thursday, cannot get the correct aid for their inner afflictions… All of it has tested me in one way or another."

To say Matthew was shocked was an understatement. He had always viewed Titus as an unflinching pillar of strength, his hardness forged through the cruelty that still marked his skin. It never crossed his mind that the same cruelty could create vulnerability, also.

"How did you fix it?" Matthew asked.

"In terms of my faith, I found my way back to God. I don't think that would be much help to you," Titus answered.

Matthew's heart sank. He felt Titus' eyes on him, watching his disappointment with a calculating gaze.

"What do you fear that you are losing faith in?" Titus asked.

"Life; the future; myself. The Holy Trinity," Matthew replied.

If Titus was bothered by the joke, it didn't show on his face. Normally, his eyebrow would have twitched at the very least. There wasn't even a glimmer of a lip curl.

"If it's life that you're losing faith in, then try to find something new in your life that could bring it back. It could be something internal or external. Faith doesn't revolve around religion. Or, at least, it doesn't have to," he explained.

Matthew chuckled softly. "I thought that you would jump at the opportunity to 'convert' me."

Titus shook his head. "My job isn't to convert you," he said. "I spread the word of God as I see fit, and that does not include forcing it on others. Where you put your faith is completely up to you and you alone. And, no, it does not have to be centred around a higher being. That's the beauty of faith. It can be in whatever you want."

Titus' words reminded Matthew of what Finn had said about modern medicine. Maybe they were right. Maybe religion wasn't the only strain of faith.

But, if this was true, what did Matthew put his faith into?

Sensing his confusion, Titus added, "You don't have to think of it on the spot. It requires deep thought and a bit of soul searching."

Matthew wasn't completely sure he even had a soul to search at this point. "Doesn't your religion dictate that I don't have a soul?"

"There are many rules written by man, not God. I refuse to accept that God would hate you. We're all his creation." Titus paused. "Besides, a soulless man would not have such an arrogant presence and way of carrying himself."

"Well, I'm certainly relieved," Matthew laughed.

"Jesus spent his time with the heathens anyway. They were the ones that needed saved."

"Oh, so what you're saying is that Jesus and I would have been best friends?"

"Well, I meant that he spent his time with the whores and the prostitutes…"

"Wait, so what you're saying is that I *am* Jesus?"

"Don't push it."

Matthew grinned. "Thanks. For the talk."

Titus surprised Matthew by smiling back. "Anytime."

~M~

"It is taking a long time for Sybil to come back," Titus murmured, nudging the blinds out of the way to peer out the window.

"Probably traffic," Thursday muttered, picking at her fingernails in the corner of the room.

"Maybe we should just call the local police," Matthew thought out loud. "I mean, we know they aren't corrupt anymore…"

"Uh-huh, and you can explain to them why we're harbouring a fugitive and have one of their own dead in our drawing room," Thursday answered.

"Surely, they would know that we had nothing to do with that"-

"Oh! And don't forget the bodies of Charles' mates in the back room too." Thursday looked up from her fingers and sighed. "Won't look suspicious at all."

Matthew huffed. "Well, we can't just sit here."

"What else do you suggest?" Sawyer boredly enquired.

"What makes you think that the Opara City Police Department are going to be more understanding than Castlebrooke's anyway?" Matthew demanded.

"Sybil has explained the situation to them. It would be a lot easier to wait for them to arrive to explain the changes than inviting a fresh set of idiots into our home," Sawyer answered.

"Is that all that you are truly concerned about, Sawyer?" Matthew asked. "More humans being in your presence?"

Sawyer grinned. "Well, now you're just putting words into my mouth."

"You are as subtle as a gun, Sawyer."

"If you say so. Go on then, call the police. See how it works out for you."

Before he could respond to that, Thursday intercepted the conversation. "If you're going to bicker, please take it somewhere else. I'm not going to sit here and listen to you both squabbling after the night I have had."

"Don't you think we should call the police, Thursday?" Matthew insisted.

Thursday shrugged. "I say we wait for Sybil. I feel like my opinion would not be given much importance considering my"- She formed a gun with her fingers and held it to her temple, pretending to shoot herself with it. Matthew guessed that it was a reference to her mental health.

"If that is true, then Sawyer shouldn't get a say, either," Matthew responded. "He has spent his fair share of time in United Arms, also."

Sawyer exhaled heavily and heaved himself to his feet. "Are we going to start dictating one another's say depending on the state of our sanity? If so, who gets to dictate what constitutes a completely sane person? *You,* Matthew? With your multiple personalities and blatant narcissism?"

Anger flared in Matthew's chest like a hot ball of fire, and he too got to his feet. "You're one to talk, Mr God Complex!"

"Oh my god, someone save me from this conversation!" Thursday shouted to the ceiling.

"No one is having their say dictated," Titus said diplomatically, turning from the blinds to face the others in the room. "The entire point of Sybil bringing us together is so that we get the opportunity to speak up and have our say. The type of opportunity we would have otherwise never received due to our differences. Now sit down the pair of you and quit embarrassing yourselves!"

Sawyer rolled his eyes. He turned towards the door as if his eyeballs steered his body. "We're waiting on Sybil," he stated, with no room for argument. It didn't even matter if anyone wanted to argue; he left before they got the chance to.

There was a brief silence that followed in his wake before Thursday spoke up. "I can't believe you just argued over who was more insane."

Matthew threw himself back into his chair and didn't answer her. He didn't understand why no one else wanted to phone the police and get this mess over with as soon as possible. Maybe they saw a flaw in the plan that he didn't see, but if they did, they sure as hell weren't making any attempt to explain it to him. He could see why waiting for Sybil seemed like the best option, but the longer they waited, the longer Ophelia was in their basement, and the longer Ophelia was in their basement, the more his skin didn't feel like it fit right.

Maybe he was being selfish. He might have desired to have Ophelia out of his home as soon as possible, which made him want to make irrational decisions. Maybe he really should just shut up and let the others do what they thought was best. He was only the shifter, after all.

"Where's Whitney?" Matthew asked despondently.

Thursday shrugged, disinterested. "Her room, I think."

"She has been having trouble with her ability," Titus clarified. "The past few days have been extremely emotionally charged, and that has been taking its toll on her. Without Sybil here... It's just been harder."

Matthew didn't know what it was that Sybil did that helped Whitney so much, but whatever it was, it worked. It could be that Sybil knew how to comfort Whitney and provide help and support, in the same way that she did for Matthew himself; Thursday; Sawyer; Titus; and, someday, Finn also.

"She hasn't been down for a whole day?"

"Nope." Thursday made a point of popping the 'p'. "I mean, I've had to roast bread over an open fire for my tea. Can you imagine? It was either that, or let Sawyer try cooking, and I am not taking *that* risk again."

Matthew frowned. "But what about Whitney? Has she been down to eat?"

"Hell, if I know," Thursday replied.

He didn't expect much more from Thursday. On a good day, Thursday remembered to attend a meal herself, never mind paying attention to other people's eating patterns. Matthew had thought that at the very least, someone else would have noticed. Judging by the look on Titus' face, though, Whitney had never crossed his mind.

Matthew had no idea how to do anything that resembled cooking, and when he made his way into the kitchen, he felt even more incompetent than he had five minutes previous. He awkwardly slapped together a sandwich. It was nothing spectacular, but at least it was edible. Or at least he hoped that it was.

Whitney's room was on the upper floor. She had insisted upon sleeping there in case an accident happened. If she set the room on fire, everyone else had a better chance of escaping. The only thing that stopped her from sleeping in the attic was how unsettled the room made her feel. Matthew wondered what she thought of Finn now residing above her. Did it make her more nervous? More afraid? More careful?

He left the sandwich and a glass of water in front of her door. He knew better than to try to go inside. Out of everyone that Whitney would want to see when she was struggling with her ability, Matthew was at the bottom of the list. He might not have even made the list at all. Instead, he gently knocked on the door and fled up the closest staircase before she answered.

Matthew hoped that she wasn't offended by the gesture. He just wanted to make sure she was looking after herself in Sybil's absence. If the slightest tilt in emotion could affect her ability, then surely being overcome with hunger would do nothing but worsen the situation. Then again, it was also entirely possible that Matthew's many skills did not include sandwich making and the deep disgust that his sandwich would cause in Whitney would cause her to become enraged and burn down Sybil's centuries-old manor.

It was just a bit of meat slapped between two slices of bread, surely there was a limit to how rage-inducing such a thing could become. No matter how shoddily made it was.

Matthew waited, not sure when he was going to risk going back down the stairs again. He wouldn't be surprised if he went down and the food was still out there. Ignoring the door was a habit Whitney had even when she wasn't spitting fire from her hands. She liked her privacy and often isolated herself instead of interacting with people. Matthew supposed he could understand that, on some level. He was Whitney's opposite, but even he sometimes wanted to be alone with his thoughts as opposed to drowning in a crowd. Instead of having that feeling occasionally, Whitney always felt it. The desire to listen to nothing but silence and the need to live in the company of oneself.

In a way, Matthew hoped that Whitney would be able to get over that. Even if she started slowly integrating herself into the company of other people, it would be a good way of getting herself out there instead of constantly being on her own. Maybe if Sybil helped her conquer her ability, it would give her the courage she needed to open herself up to others.

"What are we hiding from?"

Matthew jumped out of his skin when Finn whispered directly into his ear. He spun around, completely affronted. "Did you just sneak up on me?" he whisper-hissed back.

"If you consider walking down the stairs from my room to find you hiding here, then yeah, I was sneaking up on you," Finn replied.

Matthew forgot that he was on the stairs leading up to the attic. He shook his head, as if to clear the stupidity from his brain, and said, "Sorry, I forgot you live up there now."

Finn laughed quietly. "I will try not to take offence to that."

"Oh, you should. One hundred per cent," Matthew grinned back.

"Well, that's just lovely."

Matthew suddenly realised what this looked like. He quickly explained, "I was just leaving food out for Whitney. I didn't want her to see me, so I was hiding."

"Why do you hide from her?" Finn frowned.

"Sybil isn't here, and with all the Ophelia drama, I'm the last person she would want to see. Especially with her…" Matthew waved his hands around, hoping that it got across what he was trying to say: He didn't care to get his head blown off his shoulders.

"Not even if you were bringing her food?"

Matthew shrugged with one arm. "Whitney is the sort who likes to look after herself. I can understand that. But she's also the sort of person who would rather starve than come downstairs when her ability is like this. So, I figured I'd lend a hand. *Without* making her feel inadequate."

Finn's face softened. "That's very considerate of you."

"No, it's really not. In a way, I'm one of the very few sane people in this house right now. I must look after my family."

Matthew knew that he was far from Sybil's next in command, but with Titus keeping an eye on Thursday, and Sawyer being… *Sawyer*, someone had to step up for Whitney. Even if it was the annoying shifter with multiple personalities and narcissistic tendencies who probably made the worst sandwiches ever.

"I thought you couldn't cook?" Finn asked, quirking an eyebrow.

"I didn't exactly whip up some delicious cuisine," Matthew retaliated. "I made a sandwich."

"Ah, of course," Finn nodded. "I assume that Sybil has not returned yet, then?"

Matthew shook his head. "No, not yet. She's got to be nearly here, though. It's been a day and a half. I just hope that she's okay…"

"I'm sure she is. Sybil is an incredible woman. Even if she had encountered trouble, I'm sure she knew exactly what to do to slip out of it."

He was right. Sybil was an incredible woman. She knew how to take control of a situation, and how to lead anyone out of a problem. However, all it would take would be for her to encounter the wrong person and she could be in trouble. Not in trouble of getting hurt, but in trouble of exposing herself as telekinetic. If the people of this age could not handle the colour of Titus' skin, then surely discovering a telekinetic would bring back punishment akin to the Salem Witch trials.

In the moment's pause, Matthew swiftly analysed the man standing in front of him. That was when he noticed. "You're not using your cane."

"I can't rely on the blasted thing for the rest of my existence, can I?" Finn shrugged.

"But are you ready?"

Finn smiled. "Matthew, you don't need to worry about me. I'm a big boy, I can make these decisions myself."

Matthew reached out and enclosed the area of Finn's injured side in his hand. Finn breathed in deep, still clearly tender there, but didn't flinch away. "Is it healed?" Matthew asked curiously.

"The worst of the healing process is over, yes."

"That's a shame. I will miss you leaning against me." Matthew looked up at Finn from his place a step down. He genuinely meant it, too. Not as a flirty remark; or an indecent comment; or a quip to make Finn blush. Matthew knew that he would miss the comfortable warmth of Finn leaning his weight against him for support.

"Would you rather I hurt myself again?" Finn asked with a smirk.

Matthew blinked innocuously, pulling Finn down to his step. "Would you mind terribly?"

"Oh, of course, just let me go back to the top of these stairs and I'll chuck myself down them."

"Call it a leap of faith." Matthew captured Finn's chin between his thumb and forefinger, drawing their faces closer.

"Shut up." Finn closed the distance, and they were kissing again.

Matthew was never going to tire of this. Kissing Finn was like downing a mug of caffeine. He woke him up; revitalised him; made him feel more alive than he had ever felt before. Their lips were two jigsaw pieces that had been missing for so long, finally being fit together to complete the picture.

"I'm sorry, my lips are a bit dry," Finn said as they parted for breath.

"I wasn't going to mention it…" Matthew teased.

"Oh, shut up you."

"That's two shut-ups in two minutes. If you're not careful, you might be considered rude."

Finn stuck his hands into his back pockets, thumbs sitting on the outside of the fabric, and flicked his hair from his eyes with a jut of the head. "And what a tragedy that would be," he said, each word tinted with sarcasm.

"I'm just looking out for your social standing," Matthew said, holding his hands up in defence. "That kind of thing is extremely important these days."

"Coming from you, that's interesting," Finn said, taking a step down so that he was now shorter than Matthew. "You never struck me as the sort of man to care about societal norms."

"Lies. I'm a perfect gentleman," Matthew responded.

Finn snorted. He covered his mouth and nose with his hand as if that would somehow erase the fact that the sound had ever escaped him. Matthew rolled his eyes and slung his arm around the healer's shoulders, jumping down onto the same step as him.

"Would you like me to make you a sandwich too?" he asked.

"Since you've piqued my interest in these sandwiches, it would be rude not to," Finn answered, slowly peeling his hand back from his face when it became clear that the noise still didn't put Matthew off.

They descended the stairs together.

They had just reached the bottom when someone whizzed past them. A second later, there was a loud crash and raucous screaming. Coming straight from the place it shouldn't be: Whitney's room.

Matthew detached himself from Finn and ran out into the hall. He had only taken in the trampled sandwich and kicked over glass of water when Titus could be heard yelling from the bottom floor."

"Ophelia has escaped!"

CHAPTER FOURTEEN

Titus' voice knocked clarity into Matthew's consciousness. He could suddenly understand who was doing the screaming, and it was most certainly Ophelia Delaruse. There was no time to consider how she had escaped; the priority was to get her back to the basement before she got herself hurt. Which, since she had run straight into Whitney's bedroom, seemed to be her intention. Either that or she was extremely stupid.

"It's you, isn't it?" Ophelia was screaming. "You're the one who has taken him for yourself!"

Matthew took a step towards Whitney's room but stopped when Whitney herself slowly backed out into the hallway, her hands held up defensively. Ophelia was walking out after her, finger pointed threateningly at her chest.

"Ophelia, leave her alone!" Matthew shouted. "You don't know what you're"-

"I knew it was you the instant you answered the door!" Ophelia sneered, completely ignoring Matthew. Her eyes were wide, almost popping out of her skull, and her lip curled up in disgust. "It is always the pretty girls like you who steal away all the good men! The ones with a nice face but ugly personality!"

Whitney looked nothing but confused, the insult bouncing off her like she was wearing a suit of armour. "You don't even know me," she said.

"I get the idea of what kind of person you are," Ophelia replied. "I've met plenty of your type in my time."

Matthew inserted himself between Ophelia and Whitney. He tried to capture Ophelia's attention, but her widened eyes focused solely on the woman who was now behind him. "Ophelia, listen to me, Whitney has nothing to do with this. She is like a sister to me. If you are angry, take it out on me, not her," he insisted.

"It's her fault," Ophelia growled, trying to push her way through Matthew. "If it weren't for her"-

"Nothing would be any different! Ophelia," Matthew said firmly. She spared a glance at him, hearing the deep severity in his voice. "How did you escape?"

"United Arms couldn't hold me; do you honestly think some silly ropes could?" Ophelia answered snidely. There were deep burns around her arms from where she had struggled with the ropes, but that didn't explain how she had gotten free. The ropes should have tightened around her, not loosened.

Footsteps thundered up the stairs and Titus appeared at the top, finally reaching the floor they were on. A mere second later, Thursday jumped over the bannister in a blur of black hair and purple Glow. At their appearance, Matthew became aware of the heat on his back. Whitney.

"Don't move!" he shouted to Titus and Thursday, thrusting his hand out to stop them from taking any steps closer to them. One wrong move and Whitney could blow up. If he could get Ophelia to go willingly instead of causing a scene, it would lessen the chances of Whitney getting any more stressed than she already was.

"Yeah," Ophelia mocked. "Don't move."

"Ophelia, please, it's over. What is the point in all of this?" Matthew demanded. "No matter what you do, I'll never choose you. Especially not if you hurt any of my family."

"Family." Ophelia pulled a face. "You are as perverted as you initially thought. Changing shape and taking on aliases to sleep with people; lying so smoothly about it; and now having intercourse with your family?"

"I'm not sleeping with Whitney!" Matthew exclaimed. "Why can't you just accept the fact that I won't ever want you in that way? I can't. Why do you assume that I am sleeping with everyone?"

Ophelia narrowed her eyes darkly. "What evidence have you truly given me that you aren't?"

Matthew didn't know how else to put it. He was running out of words. "Whitney is my sister!"

"You're a liar and a manipulator, Matthew. How am I even supposed to believe you when you say that?" Ophelia demanded to know.

"*I'm* a liar? What about *you?*" Matthew bit back. "That letter you wrote to Samuel was very convincing. That 'my husband is going to kill me' act was also very impressive."

"I was admitted to an asylum," Ophelia smirked. "What is your excuse?" Her face curled with revulsion, and she looked down. "What am I standing in?" she shouted.

"It's a sandwich," Matthew answered flatly. "I brought it up for Whitney."

"What?" he heard Whitney say behind him.

Ophelia rubbed her shoe against the beige carpet, trying to remove the bread and butter from the sole. When that didn't work, she huffed and returned her glare to Matthew. "You could admit yourself to the asylum. They would gladly take you, I'm sure. Try to cure you of all your perversions. Incest; sexual promiscuity; that awful indecency that you're afflicted with."

"Indecency?"

"Oh please, don't even pretend you don't know. Don't you realise that it is obvious?" Ophelia tutted. "It's perfectly clear that you're one of those filthy sodomit"-

Whitney grabbed Matthew by the arms and threw him out of her way. He didn't hear the end of Ophelia's sentence, nor did he have a chance to get angry at the implication of the slur that was about to be thrown at him. All he registered was the ground rushing towards him and a sharp burn on his biceps from where Whitney had touched him.

"Take that back." Whitney had Ophelia by the front of her dress. Her face twisted into an infuriated snarl. "Take that back right now."

"Whitney, it's okay," Matthew said carefully, getting to his knees slowly.

"No, it's not," Whitney growled. "This woman has been throwing her weight around, screaming at all of us for taking you from her and now she dares to call you that? Not in my presence, do you hear me?" She shook Ophelia, causing her to yelp in surprise.

Matthew was painfully aware of Whitney's hands, which were slowly beginning to glow, like the embers of a fire before they flared into life. "Whitney, please, step away"-

"We took you in!" Whitney screamed into Ophelia's face. "We helped you! We let you into our home! We saved your sorry ass from Charles! We didn't have to do any of that! And this is how you repay us? Insulting us? Trying to kill us? Why are you all the same? Why do all you people just take and take and take and take? What do we have to do to earn your respect!"

Ophelia finally looked afraid. It could have been Whitney's words that triggered this; or the look on her face; or the fact that her hands were increasing in heat by the second.

"Whitney," Matthew reached out with a trembling hand and placed it on her shoulder. His heart was pounding in his chest, the fear of what could happen if Whitney's anger increased battering his ribcage like the blows of a hammer. "Whitney. Listen to me. Take a deep breath. You need to calm down."

Whitney was trembling harder than Matthew was. Her breathing was sharp and haggard, like an asthmatic who had just run a mile without having smoked some Stramonium beforehand. She was crying, but the tears were evaporating off her skin as soon as they escaped her eyelids.

"Yes, Whitney, you need to calm down," Ophelia growled mockingly.

"Do you want to die?" Matthew snapped at the woman. "She will kill us all and it will be your fault!"

"If I concentrate," Whitney said through gritted teeth. "I may be able to only kill her."

Matthew was forced to remove his hand due to the sheer heat that was emanating from Whitney's body. His palm immediately began to sting from the burn, but he ignored it for the moment. "But do you want to?" he asked gently.

"She called you"-

"I know what she called me. It's okay."

"No, it's not!"

"We're going to be called a lot of things, Whitney. I've endured worse. Please, let her go," Matthew implored.

"She doesn't deserve to live," Whitney growled.

"We don't get to decide that, annoyingly." Matthew knew that deep down, Whitney did not want to kill Ophelia. Not like this. Not because she lost control. He just didn't know how to communicate that to her. "Look, whatever you decide to do, I'll stand by you, but please think about it. Just for a moment."

The silence that followed was so thick that it felt like it was sticking to Matthew's throat with every breath he took. Whitney's fists were shaking as she clutched the front of Ophelia's dress desperately, the fabric blackened like the bottom of a pan. At that moment, Matthew could not tell which way things were going to swing. Like building blocks that had been built too high, he didn't know in what direction they were going to topple.

Whitney thrust Ophelia into the closest wall and turned into Matthew. The second her body touched him, he was shocked by the cold, but he didn't care. He wrapped his arms around her. As they stood like that, water slowly began to dampen Matthew's clothes. It was seeping off Whitney onto him.

"I hate you," Whitney muttered into his chest.

Matthew laughed. "I know," he answered.

"Come on." Thursday grabbed Ophelia and all but threw her at the staircase. She would have toppled down them if Titus had not caught her in time. "Back to the basement with you."

Whitney stepped back from Matthew. She was sopping wet, her clothes soaked straight through. She was looking at a point over his shoulder, clearly embarrassed by the vulnerability she had just put on display. Matthew wanted to ask if she was okay, but he didn't know if she would take kindly to it. Whitney was a hard person to read.

Folding her arms together, she nodded at Matthew silently and turned to go back into her room.

"Whitney, wait," Matthew said, catching her hand.

"What?" Whitney replied, green eyes defensive.

"Promise me you'll eat something."

Her gaze immediately softened. She looked at the mess on the floor that had once been her sandwich, and she nodded. "I promise."

Matthew smiled and released her hand. "Thank you."

Whitney nodded at him again and went into her room, closing the door between them.

Matthew ran an exhausted hand over his face. He picked up the glass and plate and headed for the stairs. He would have to get a brush and pan to clean up the mess Ophelia had made. At least she had not broken the dishes. There was something positive right there. Right?

When he reached the top of the stairs, someone took the dishes out of his hands. Alarmed, Matthew turned to see who it was and felt stupid when he saw Finn. Of course, it was only Finn. Who the hell else would it have been?

No words passed between them. Finn slid his hand into Matthew's, and he was overcome with relief. Matthew released a breath as Finn healed the burn that had scorched his palm. Of course, it hadn't left a mark, but Matthew had been able to feel its effect, nonetheless.

Matthew and Finn walked down the stairs, hand in hand. They did not let go. Not when Thursday and Titus emerged from the basement on the bottom floor; not when Sawyer conveniently returned through the back door when all the trouble was over. This was what they wanted.

They did not care what anyone else thought.

CHAPTER FIFTEEN

"How do you think she escaped?"

Matthew couldn't take his eyes off Ophelia as she stood in handcuffs at the door, jabbering nonsense about being Charles' wife and how if they just contacted him, they would know that she was innocent. When Charles' body was wheeled past her out to the ambulance, she declared, "There he is, just ask him!"

To make things run a lot more smoothly, Sybil pinned the deaths of Charles' friends on Ophelia also. It wouldn't affect much of her sentence; either way, she was going to be escorted straight back to United Arms and never let out again. Matthew felt a tinge of sadness at the thought of the woman he had once admired reduced to such a bleak fate. Then he remembered how she was a murderer and very, very insane.

But weren't the seven of them the same?

"Matthew?"

Matthew shook out of his reverie and focused on Sybil. She had arrived early the following morning with the Opara City Police Department. They were informed of what had happened while they were not there and once briefed, they took control of the situation entirely. He and Sybil now sat side by side on the staircase, having watched everything unfold in the foyer.

"Sorry, I was somewhere else. What did you say?" Matthew asked.

"I asked how you think she escaped?" Sybil replied.

Matthew had pondered the same question all night. He had not slept well at all, haunted by how close Whitney had come to losing control. The one thing from what had happened that still did not add up was how Ophelia had escaped in the first place. Thursday had tied her down, and she was not the sort of person to slack on her knots.

"I don't know. Her arms are burned, so she must have struggled," Matthew answered. He shrugged. "Still makes no sense, though."

Sybil blew an exhausted raspberry. "I'm so glad she didn't provoke Whitney like she had intended." She touched Matthew's arm. "Thanks to you, we are all still intact."

"Thanks to Whitney, more like," Matthew corrected. "She is getting better at controlling herself."

Sybil smiled, pride beaming from every crease on her face. "She is," she said. Her expression turned stern. "It was a bad judgment call to allow Ophelia to stay here. I will have to be more careful in future."

"If it weren't for me, she would never have found us," Matthew sighed, propping his chin on his hand.

Sybil mimicked Matthew's stance, placing her elbow on her knee to support her arm and head. "I suppose we could spend the rest of our lives trying to find blame in ourselves," she murmured. "And that is a pretty long time, all things considered."

This made Matthew chuckle. "Yes, you are probably right."

They watched Ophelia be led away by the police. She tried to catch Matthew's eye as the door was pulled closed, but he looked away before she could. He had had enough of staring into those eyes. He never wanted to see them again.

"It was probably just dumb luck that she escaped," Sybil said, breaking the silence that had followed.

Matthew was relieved that the police were all gone because repeating the same statement a thousand times grew extremely old extremely fast. The authorities had an overbearing presence that made it feel like they were invading Matthew's space. He wished that they could just take the culprit and the bodies and leave. But, no, that was not how the protocol worked anymore.

"Yeah, dumb luck that almost got the house burnt down," Matthew joked dryly.

Sybil's eyebrows drew together. Hearing it come from someone else's mouth had changed her perspective. "Luck. . ."

"Are they gone?" Sawyer asked, appearing at the top of the stairs. Before either of them could answer, he had flown down and pulled Sybil to her feet. His hair was pinned up by two quills, a new look for him. Nice that he had time to develop a fresh style while the rest of them were dealing with the police. "Sybil, darling, I'm delighted that you returned safely." He embraced her tightly.

Sybil was weirdly silent. As if sensing her odd behaviour, Sawyer released her from his grasp. He held onto her shoulders; concern etched over his features. "What is it?" he asked.

"I want to talk to you, Sawyer," Sybil said sternly, shrugging his hands off her. "Come with me."

Sawyer followed Sybil out into the kitchen. If Matthew had to guess, Sybil was taking him to the back garden where their conversation wouldn't be heard. He could only resist the temptation to follow for half a minute, which was thankfully plenty of time to put enough distance between him and them.

Matthew was surprised to find Thursday in the kitchen. She was sitting on the bench closest to the sink, attempting to peel a potato. When she noticed Matthew, she grinned. "I figured since Whitney has been going through so much, I'd attempt to do this again," she said.

Her expression changed from joking to serious when Matthew ignored her and went straight to the back door. He was careful not to lean too hard against it. Titus and Finn had repaired it as best they could, but they weren't carpenters. Too much pressure and it would break off its hinges again.

Sybil was yelling at Sawyer, just far enough down the garden for her words to be indistinguishable. Sawyer didn't look bothered by Sybil's shouting, but when did he ever? The sunlight bathed the pair in a yellow glow. The golden rays favoured them as if Mother Nature wished to highlight their dispute to onlookers.

What had happened? Had Matthew missed something?

Sybil's attitude changed when Ophelia had been led out of the house. When she had commented on dumb luck. What had caused the shift in mood? Matthew wanted to think that it was just the sight of Sawyer's face that made her turn so sour so fast, but he knew that was not the truth, even if he wanted it to be.

It clicked so suddenly that Matthew almost knocked his face against the windowpane.

Luck. Of course. Stupid; dumb; irrational luck.

Ophelia had escaped from her ropes because Sawyer had influenced fate to make it happen.

Anger hit Matthew like a car. He wanted to charge out and scream at Sawyer too. Say his piece; make the man feel like the pathetic person that he was, to yell and yell and yell some more until it finally sunk in for Sawyer that he was a sorry excuse for a man who had not only risked their lives but risked the safety of their homestead. All for the sake of what? What had he wanted to achieve?

Sybil had started pointing to the gates at the bottom of the garden, silently shouting what Matthew could discern as *"Go! Go now! Go! Get out of my sight!"*

Sawyer lifted his hands in submission and sauntered away from Sybil. He exited the grounds like a man going on a jaunt, not a man who had just had his ears screamed off and been kicked out of his home. Sybil turned her back on him and shielded her eyes with her hand. She stared at the ground as if she could find guidance there.

"He'll be back."

Matthew started at Thursday's sudden presence behind him. She was just as good as Finn at appearing and disappearing behind him without making a single sound.

"What makes you think so?" Matthew muttered.

"Sybil couldn't abandon any of us. Even when we do wrong, she wants to help. It's her weakness," Thursday answered. "Yeah, Sawyer will be back. I'm sure he knows that he will be too."

Of course, she was right. There was no way that Sybil would abandon Sawyer. She wouldn't abandon any of them. She couldn't. Matthew supposed that everyone had to have one, even her. Finn couldn't heal himself; Whitney's control over nature was dictated by her emotions; and Sybil couldn't leave anyone behind. This knowledge didn't make it feel any better.

"Can you believe that he did that?" Matthew growled through clenched teeth.

He could see Thursday's reflection in the windowpane. She sighed heavily. "Yes, I can," she answered honestly. "We should have known. At the very least I should have guessed. It never crossed my mind."

"It didn't cross anyone's mind. I thought that he would have the sense not to cross such a line, so I didn't even think to consider it." Matthew felt incredibly stupid. Why had he thought that Sawyer would be fine with a human being in their home? Why did he think for one second that he would respect Sybil's wishes to get the police involved? Of course, he wouldn't. Sawyer didn't respect anyone's authority but his own.

Sybil's shoulders were shaking. Matthew opened the door and went to her. She was covering her face, trying to hide that she was upset, but reached for him as he came close and accepted his hug. As if closing the curtain on a performance, a dark cloud passed over them, plunging them into its shade.

"Why must he do this to us?" she cried. "Why does he always do this to us?"

"I don't know Sybil," Matthew said into her hair. "I really don't know."

Fury raged through Matthew's blood. The same fury that always lay dormant in the pit of his stomach, constantly awakened by Sawyer and his refusal to accept any form of help. He had something wrong with him. To have come from a life of hardship and to be welcomed into a massive home and given a family, and yet still choose to wreck and disrespect the very people who gave him this life? Even Thursday wasn't that insane.

Matthew wished that Sawyer would understand what he did to them. What he had done to Whitney last night and the chaos it could have caused. What he had done to Sybil, the only woman who still tried to see the good in him. What he did to this family regularly without seeming to give it a second thought.

When he opened his eyes and looked up from Sybil's head, Matthew saw Thursday watching them from the doorway.

—280—

He couldn't decipher the expression on her face. That wasn't strange. When Thursday didn't want to be read, she wouldn't be read.

"I need to go after him," Sybil hiccupped, pulling out of Matthew's arms. "I need to bring him back. Who knows what kind of danger he could put himself in? Or put others in."

"Sybil…"

"No, I must. He's dangerous. He proved that today, didn't he?"

"Sybil," Matthew started, "please"-

"Don't try to talk me out of it, Matthew. Whatever you want to say, I know." Sybil sniffed. "Trust me, *I know.*"

Matthew chose not to argue with her. He could see the hurt in her eyes. The gaping wound that Sawyer's betrayal had left reflected in the glistening tears on her lower lids. She wiped the tears from her eyes, wiping the evidence of her sorrow away. A pillar of strength, slightly jilted, slowly fixing their mask to ensure that no one saw the cracks in their mask.

"Sybil." Thursday joined them, winding an arm around Sybil's shoulders. "Don't go after him. He will come back on his own. Let him grovel for his bed tonight."

"I don't know if that is such a good id"-

"No buts. He's going to grovel like he has never grovelled before." Thursday started guiding Sybil back to the house and out of the cold. "Whitney needs you more right now. Let's go check on her."

Matthew watched the two women return to the house. He was glad that Thursday had jumped in. She was a lot calmer about the situation than he was, and calm was what Sybil needed right now. Matthew was bristling with anger and would not have been much help to her. No matter what he said, Sybil would still allow Sawyer back into the house, and all it would have resulted in was a shouting match.

It could not be put into words how frustrating it was that Sybil would not let Sawyer go. Even now, when he put everyone at risk, he would not be gone for long. It made Matthew wonder what it would take for Sybil to finally decide that enough was enough. Would Sawyer have to kill someone before she saw what he truly was? Sybil always looked too much at the potential in people; what they could be in the future instead of what they are now. She was so busy trying to fix people that she didn't seem to consider the possibility that maybe some people were unfixable.

But, in the same breath, Matthew depended on Sybil for the same leniency. If she had chosen to, she could have thrown him out for jeopardizing their safety by leaving their address where Ophelia could find it. He had put Ophelia in danger by unintentionally putting her in Whitney's line of fire. The whole reason that Ophelia was there in the first place was because of him. Instead of flying off the handle (albeit, she had given him an earful, which was fair enough) Sybil had taken the situation into her hands and tried to find a solution.

Who would have thought that the lives of the cursed would be anything but easy?

"Okay, okay, I'm going, stop pushing me-*hey*!"

Matthew looked over his shoulder. Finn had stumbled out the back door, having been pushed out by Thursday, whose smug smirk was clear through the window as she threw the door shut again.

Upon noticing that Matthew had seen him being thrust out by Thursday, Finn's face flushed. "Ah, a little birdie told me that you were needing company," he said.

Matthew smiled sadly. "Did that birdie have black hair and a Spanish accent?"

Finn approached him. He shrugged. "Possibly." As soon as he was within distance, he took Matthew's hands in both of his. "Are you okay?"

"Would you believe me if I said yes?" Matthew asked.

"Possibly."

"Then, yes, I'm okay."

"I don't believe you."

Matthew laughed emptily. "Why can't everything be so much simpler?"

Finn was stroking the top of Matthew s hand with his thumb, and it was incredibly distracting. With every stroke, Matthew felt more at ease. "If life was easy, then it would be very boring. These challenges are given to us to test us. We usually come out of it having learned something about ourselves. Or about others."

"So, I can say that I have learned that Sawyer is a pathetic little rat of a man who doesn't deserve this family?" Matthew enquired.

"Did you not already know that?"

Matthew shook his head, but a smile was threatening to tug at his lips. "Whitney could have hurt Ophelia. She could have killed us all."

Finn closed his eyes. "I know," he said.

"Why would he do that to her?" Matthew asked these questions knowing that Finn didn't have the answers. He just needed someone to throw his thoughts at. The only person who would know the answers was Sawyer himself and the sun would freeze over before he would ever let such secrets slip.

"Some people aren't worth trying to understand," Finn said. "Maybe, someday, Sawyer will change. Maybe, someday, he will see what he has and realise that the wrong move at the wrong time could cause him to lose it all. I know that that is the glimmer of hope that Sybil is hanging onto, and maybe she's foolish for that, or maybe she is doing something that none of us have the strength to do ourselves."

"And what's that?" Matthew asked.

Finn's hands tightened around Matthew's. "She sees the good in people. She sees something in Sawyer that we can't see."

"I can't imagine what."

"That's the point." Finn shrugged with one arm. "She puts her faith in people."

Matthew didn't know if he should feel better or worse about that. It made sense that Sybil would put her faith in her family, even if they constantly betrayed her trust and tore her down. In a way, it made Matthew angrier. For someone to betray such faith and trust, to do it with that ridiculous self-satisfied smirk that Sawyer always wore… There weren't words for how that made Matthew feel.

"Sawyer will reap what he sows," Finn added.

Matthew shook his head in disbelief. "He controls fate."

"There are some things even Sawyer can't control."

"I find that hard to believe."

"Sawyer needs help," said Finn.

Matthew scoffed. "Sawyer is beyond anything that could resemble help."

"At least no one was hurt. That's what we must focus on."

Matthew knew that Finn was right, but that did nothing to smother his anger. He felt like he was the only person who was truly bothered by what Sawyer did. Sybil was going to allow him back and in a few weeks' time everyone would be acting like nothing had ever happened.

"Maybe Sawyer will apologise?" Finn suggested. "To Whitney, I mean."

Finn's naivety made Matthew laugh bitterly. "Sawyer won't apologise. That's not how he operates."

"He might. He seems to care about this family. He harmed Whitney in his endeavour to hurt Ophelia. He could recognise that and seek Whitney's forgiveness."

Matthew could see what Finn was trying to say, but he didn't see that happening. Sawyer didn't feel remorse. Matthew would be surprised if it was even a concept that Sawyer was familiar with. He was almost convinced that most emotions that the madman displayed were not real. A folly. A ruse. Like he was imitating behaviour that he knew was considered normal.

It was then at times like this when the act didn't work. Where his mark of normality slipped, and he acted how *he* saw fit. Never mind what was conventional, Sawyer would do what Sawyer thought was right. It was a look into the man's psyche that Matthew had never wanted.

Of course, this was all purely speculation. Matthew felt like he wasn't far from the truth, though.

Who knew what the truth was? Sometimes Matthew believed that he was the only person who thought that Sawyer needed to be constantly watched. Or, at the very least, be checked up on periodically. Wasn't what happened last night an example of this?

Finn cast his eyes to the ground, seeing that there was nothing he could say that would make Matthew feel better about what happened. Matthew knew that that was why Thursday had pushed him out into the garden in the first place. He wondered if Finn would always come when he was upset. He was so used to keeping it bottled and hidden, that Matthew didn't know what it felt like to have someone ready and willing to stay by his side when he was sad.

"I accept."

Matthew blinked. "I'm sorry?"

"Your formal expression of interest. I accept." Finn was still looking at the ground, too nervous to meet Matthew's gaze.

"You're not just saying that because I've been upset?" Matthew asked sceptically, his heart having picked up several notches.

Finn shook his head. "I'm saying it because I think you're amazing. You care so much and try so hard, even when you feel upset or neglected." He inhaled deeply, his voice shaking as he murmured, "And you're so gorgeous."

Being complimented was something that Matthew had grown familiar with long ago. His shifting ability meant that he received them regularly. He was used to them being superficial, based solely on his appearance and nothing more. Matthew had always believed that it was his burden to bear. Each one of The Seven had a cross to carry concerning their abilities and, inconvenience aside, Matthew had always figured that his was that nobody would love him for who he was.

Yet here was a man who not could see him for who he truly was and liked what he saw. Finn could see into him; had observed how he acted daily; had witnessed him weep and mourn and curse his existence. Through all that anger, sadness, and dirt, he had somehow found something worth standing by. Something that he *wanted* to stand by.

It made Matthew feel raw. Every compliment that came from Finn was in a completely different league from any meaningless drivel he had ever received before. He felt himself blush for what was to be the first time in his life.

"Are you sure?" he asked. "People tire of me very quickly. You don't know what you're getting yourself into."

"I can safely say that I will not tire of you," Finn confidently replied. It was his turn to blush as he added, "You make me happy."

It was such a simple statement, but it held so much importance. Happiness, above all else, was what Matthew wished for the people he cared about. If only there would be a way for his siblings to be happy, then he would have nothing to worry about. The fact that he made Finn happy, without even really trying, meant so much to him. After all that Finn had endured, he deserved every ounce of happiness he could get. A service which Matthew was more than happy to provide.

"You have tipped my entire world on its end," Matthew said. "I hope you realise that."

Finn's lips tightened with worry. "Is that a good thing?"

Matthew grinned; the gesture so genuine he had put no effort into it. "It is an amazing thing."

Finn's shoulders relaxed. "Is that a yes?" he asked.

"A yes to your yes?" Matthew raised his eyebrows. "Accepting your acceptance of my offer? How complex."

"Just answer me, you buffoon."

Matthew lifted their joined hands and nodded. "Of course, I am saying yes."

Finn let out such a loud sigh of relief that it made Matthew's smile widen. The healer rested his forehead against their clasped hands. No more words were needed. As if a huge weight had been lifted off his shoulders, Matthew let his head fall forward and rest against Finn's.

Contentment fit like a glove.

This was what belonging felt like. Holding someone's hand and feeling complete; having a home to defend; a family to protect. It was hard, and sometimes it hurt, and a lot of the time it felt pointless, but you do it anyway. This was what Matthew had been looking for his entire life, and despite how dangerous and messy and difficult their abilities made things, he would not have it any other way.

About the Author

Erin Curran is an unapologetically queer, neurodivergent writer from Northern Ireland. Having fostered a passion for creative writing at a young age, Erin is rarely seen without two things: a cup of tea and a pen. She won the English Millennium Cup in High School and went on to have her now self-published novel, The Seven, longlisted for a GALA award in 2020. Her goal as an author is to contribute to normalising LGBTQIA+ characters and stories, bringing them into the mainstream where they belong. When not writing, Erin is either reading; drawing; video editing or listening to Queen. Not necessarily in that order.

Printed in Great Britain
by Amazon